T0164771

Enter The Heart

By:

Ben Romen

Order this book online at www.trafford.com
or email orders@trafford.com

Most Trafford titles are also available at major online book retailers.

Printed in the United States of America.

ISBN: 978-1-4269-7902-6 (sc)
ISBN: 978-1-4269-7903-3 (e)

Library of Congress Control Number: 2011912372

Trafford rev. 07/16/2011

 www.trafford.com

North America & international
toll-free: 1 888 232 4444 (USA & Canada)
phone: 250 383 6864 ♦ fax: 812 355 4082

Chapter I

I WANTED TO SAY HELLO

I was in a little coffee house in Milan, Italy. I had been drinking coffee and listening to an Italian accent, which had a funny sound to it. It took me a moment to recognize what kind of accent it was. Hearing Italian spoken with a foreign accent is a common thing in Milan. It was the Brooklyn accent that had caught my ear and intrigued me. She was chatting with another woman. I wanted to say hello and find out who she was and how she came to be here in Milan.

I figured that if I strolled over to her table and said hello with a Brooklyn accent, even if it was faked, she might think I was from Brooklyn. She would be glad to say hello to someone from the same old neighborhood. Then after the ice was broken I would drop the phony accent and explain where I was really from and that I had just wanted to say hello. By then my charm would have won her attention. She would smile and laugh lightly. We would engage in small talk and enjoy our coffee. She would be captivated by my American coolness. We would be in bed together soon, maybe even tonight. So went my thoughts.

I strolled over to her table, looked down at her in my best command performance presence profile, smiled my charming casual smile and said, "Hi! Don't I know you? You's from Brooklyn; ain't ya?"

Her face went pale and slack. She seemed to have trouble getting her breath. For a brief moment, I thought she was choking on something. She grabbed her handbag from off the table and stood up in one sudden motion and disappeared out of the coffee house and into the street traffic.

It happened so suddenly that I was standing there with my practiced casual smile sliding down my face into an open mouthed gape. I wasn't expecting that reaction. I realized that I must look stupid, standing there by the vacated chair staring at the door. Her friend got up, looked at me quizzically and left. It took an effort to close my mouth. Suddenly, feeling self conscious, I made my way to the door and my escape into the street.

I had about forgotten about her when about a week later I saw her in a women's hair salon. She was working there. She was doing something to a woman's hair that only women understand. I moved away from in front of the window.

I still wanted to meet her and learn her story. Yeah, well Ok, the rest of the truth is, she was very

attractive. Her face wasn't beautiful, but its features were nicely balanced and attractive. Her body was trim. She didn't have large breasts, but when my eyes followed her silhouette from neck to knee, the curves were all there, and in a very pleasing ratio too.   So, all right, you've figured out what it really was that attracted me to want to meet her in the first place. Her accent was just what had caught my attention in the coffee house and made me look at her. It was after that look, that I
decided that I should say hello.

You see, I like women. Since I've been on this trip, that's about two weeks now, I haven't had one in my arms, let alone in my bed. Now don't get me wrong. I am an attractive enough guy, but sometimes women don't realize that right off. So anyway, sometimes I need to get close to them before they notice me.

I would like to have a chance with this woman, if I could just find some opportunity to put myself into her world. After all, we were both Americans in Italy. I figured it should be a natural cinch. She had to be Italian American. She obviously lived here, but she could only have come by that accent by growing up in Brooklyn. That made me curious, but then there was also that line; that curving line of her body's I had mentioned. At her waist, the curve actually pinched inward, not out like so many. I don't know what there is about that line, but I'll tell you this; when I look at it, I get this primal feeling, low down in my body, that feels pretty good. And I'm not speaking about my stomach either. The more I studied her lines the stronger the feeling was growing. I wanted to wrap my arms around that waist and draw that profile close to my profile, if you know what I mean.

From across the street, at a sidewalk café, I could see through the beauty shop's window and still not look like I was watching. She wasn't visible all the time, but I was very much enjoying the occasional view of her silhouette.

I don't know why I had never noticed it before. It was when I was seeing her shadowy profile through the window that I realized; that what was making my body yearn for her wasn't so much large breasts or a well-formed leg. It was her waist. Her waist accented her female form. Her waist emphasized the swell of her breasts and the swell of her hips. As I was appreciating her swells I was getting a swelling feeling myself. Spying on her, from across the street made me feel sleazy, besides it wasn't satisfying to just look at her.

I think I can understand how some of those sick guys started to get obsessed with some woman and took to stalking her. That thought made me feel real uncomfortable about myself. I'm not going to become one of those sick puppies. I'm going to go over there, meet her, be direct, but I don't want to freak her out again.

First, I have to figure an angle on this. She works in a women's beauty salon. Therefore, I can not just stroll in and 'accidentally' recognize her and say, "Oh hi! Say, I'm sorry about startling you the other day. You reminded me of someone else and…." Forget about it! That won't work. I've got to come up with something else. I'm not going to stroll into a women's shop. Maybe when the shop closes, I could follow her to see where else she goes and find a more comfortable place to 'bump into her'. Yeah, that might work.

Then, it dawned on me. What if she has a boy friend pick her up at work or a husband? Damn! That idea struck me and I felt myself angry at the thought that someone else had a claim on her. Damn again! Why hadn't I thought about that before?

A waiter had asked me if I wanted anything else. I muttered, "Prego!" I had been so involved with my thoughts that I had not realized that I had drunk my coffee. I was surprised at my self. I'm feeling jealous over a woman I don't know and who may be married. I should just forget about her and find myself someone else.

Someone was saying something to me, loudly, and with a bit of anger in their voice. As I came out of my reverie, I looked up. It was she and she had anger on her face like one of those Hawaiian Tike dolls. I had been here to watch her and done such a piss poor job of it that not only had she seen me, but now she had walked right over to my table and I hadn't even noticed.

"Just who the hell are you and why are you spying on me? Are you working for Little Joe? What do you want?" Her questions were popping off like a string of firecrackers. "How long have you been following me?" She paused to catch a little air. My turn to talk. "Oh! Hi! Gee, I'm sorry about startling you the other day. You reminded me of someone and…" I'm sounding pretty lame here, I thought. There was no time to come up with something that would sound suave and besides--I had been caught.

I stopped talking, took a slow breath and started again. "Ok! Ok! I was watching you just now, but I haven't been following you. This is the first time I've seen you since I fumbled while trying to say hello last week. Which reminds me. Why did you run out of there so abruptly?

Did I have spinach in my teeth or something? I was just trying to say hello. I know I'm not Wayne Newton, but you reacted like you had just seen Dracula." I paused and waited for her to explain.

"That's a lie! How did you know where I worked if you had not been following me? You even know which table I prefer to sit at when I take my coffee break." She paused and glared the Tiki face at me.

Oh great, I thought. That is just great. Not only did I not have my attention on watching her, but I had tried watching her from a table, she thought of as being hers. I'm not too good at this sneaking around and spying on people business. Welding is a whole lot simpler. I can predict how the metal is going to react to the heat, but this woman; who could predict this?

I started laughing at my predicament and myself. The situation had become absurd. I said, "Your table! This is your table?" I laughed at my mental image of Stan Laurel saying, "This is another fine mess you've managed to get us into."

I stood up and told her, "Look, I just passed by and saw you. I sat down here while trying to think of someway to say hello, but now I'm not sure I want to meet you. You seem to be angry with me every time I run into you. Good-bye!"

I began to stride away with dignity. The waiter hustled over. "Signore! Signore!" He was holding out the bill for the coffee. I had to halt my grand exit to dig into my pocket for the change. After fumbling through two pockets I was able to get the sum together. I thought, I couldn't even escape a scene with dignity.

She didn't say another word. She just kept an angry pouting look on her face. I thought her look might even have had some disdain in it. Disdain! Yeah, that is what it was. So, that is what disdain looks like. I had read the word somewhere, back a few months ago. I didn't know what it meant. I had looked it up in my dictionary. The definition seemed a little vague to me. Then, I saw it on her face. Now I understood the word. Ugh! It wasn't pretty.

I was uncomfortable with the feeling that I was disdainful. I don't interface with people a lot in my work. I am a welder. The extent to which I interact with people on the job is when my foreman tells me what he needs me to do that day. I then set about doing it. That is about it.

For the last eighteen months I had been working on an oil well drilling platform in the North Sea. It was a brand new platform design, just coming out of the water, and there had been a lot of us with long days and little rest. We had just completed getting the deck down and now a few of us could be spared for a little vacation time. The number of working hours in a day backed off to ten. I spend most of my working time 'under the hood'. Which is what we call it when we are working, wearing our welding hood. My vision is limited to the welding bead I'm putting down and the noise doesn't invite polite conversation. I have to pay close attention to the details of what I'm doing for long hours, everyday, for months at a time. It isn't that I'm antisocial. It is rather, that I'm unskilled at small talk. I might enjoy your company, to go fishing or hunting, but let's just not talk about it. You see, I'm still learning how to communicate well with words.

It is difficult to even to admit to having feelings let alone talking about them. I think it goes back to the way I was raised. I like my work, but it isn't conducive to developing social skills.

We have built a little bar in the workers quarters. We can have a few beers and a little talk at the end of the day. I tried it for a while, but my liver cannot live with the amount of brew, most of these guys are pouring down their throats. The talk is always about the job or women. So, I spend the couple of hours I have between work, eating, and sleeping with reading.

The characters in the books I read are my social contacts. I read everything I can get a hold of. There are quite a few paperbacks, which circulate around. The subject matter runs the gamut from Snoopy and The Red Baron to All The President's Men; from Barbara Cortland to Dilbert; from Playboy's articles about Sex In The Age of Aids to The Static and Dynamic Stresses Induced into Stainless Steel Piping by Plasma Welding. I'm a very well read guy. Just ask me about anything. I have read either something about it or I will soon and I'll have an opinion about it too.

Every six months we can catch a helicopter ride out of here and connect with the rest of the world for a few weeks. I usually look forward to meeting a woman, developing a lasting, in depth friendship over a couple of hours and then sharing some quality time together in the sack. It might surprise you to find out, how seldom this really happens. I usually have a few beers, try to strike up an interesting conversation, and spend the night alone. Maybe I should learn how to dance. Women are frustrating to try to figure out.

After a night or two of this I usually end up visiting some old world city and marveling at the architecture. I can stick steel together with weld and span great spans, but the only material any of the old masters had was stone. I am awe struck when I gaze upon some of these monuments to man's engineering and building prowess. I am thrilled within my soul when I look at the grandeur of so many of the old buildings.

I had chosen Milan for this vacation. It was February and the weather there was much better than that in the North Sea. I had eight more days to enjoy the beautiful old city. I wasn't about to waste more of my precious time on some 'dingbat', as Archie Bunker might have called her.

A drenching rain had begun to fall and I holed up in a little restaurant and wine bar. I was savoring a semi-sweet red wine when she ran in from the rain with a co-worker. I knew that the other woman was a co-worker from the identical smock. They were sharing a laugh over something. I don't know why I did it, but I walked over and said, "Hello again! Can we talk this time or are we going to snarl and spit at each other?"

In one motion, she looked at her co-worker, the heavy rain, and me. For a moment, I thought she was going to head back out into it. She seemed to resign herself to the idea of saying hello. She ordered her wine, glared at me through her rain soaked hair and spoke. "Maybe you are not a cold blooded professional. You are just a hot-blooded, inept man who is trying much too hard at being a jerk." She continued to glare at me over the rim of her glass as she sipped her wine and I thought I could see that she was gloating over her smooth put down of me.

I could only say, "Yes! Well, like I said, hello. Note! I was here first. I did not follow you in here." I never was any good at one-line put-downs. I didn't rehearse them like some people do. Right then I wished I had one, but I didn't. I saw that I wasn't going to continue this conversation, so I just raised my glass as some sort of salute and returned to my table.

The bar continued to fill up with people escaping the rain. The women were talking and had not noticed that all the tables were quickly taken. I had intentionally turned my back to them and was actively sizing up the other ladies in the bar. She walked over to me and spoke to my back, "So, What d-ya wanna talk about anyway?" Her Brooklyn English was so raw; I was tempted to tell her to put it back in the oven and let it finish baking. I changed my mind and didn't say a word about it. Now it was my turn to be cool and aloof, but I didn't do that either. I wasn't in the mood to play games, so I just let myself be me. I turned around and just said, "Hello! My name is Jim. I am an American, on vacation. You are welcome to sit and get acquainted if you wish."

After our glasses were empty, I ordered a carafe for the table. After another glass, we ordered some food. Actually, she ordered for us, in Italian. It was some pasta and seafood dish, which I didn't know about. It was great. The conversation had softened and after awhile had become somewhat pleasant, even friendly. I was enjoying myself. I think she was also. I could tell by the way she smiled. It wasn't the Tiki face anymore. She told me her name was Annette. I called her Annie. She said that was better than being called mouseketeer.

The rain had ceased and Rosa, the co-worker, left for home. I asked Annie to have dessert with me. I ordered another glass to wash down the dessert. We were both feeling much more relaxed and comfortable with each other after having become better acquainted. I think those glasses must have been undersize, because they ran out so quickly.

I was ready to order another glass, but Annie said she wanted to see if I could dance. I let her drag me to some dance bar down the street. After a couple of hours of dancing, and downing a few more glasses of wine, she was getting very relaxed. I was enjoying holding that very nice curvaceous body snuggly against mine as we moved. She was enjoying the dancing and the holding too. Sometimes I could feel a shudder run through her as we moved our hips against one another. I was getting hard and she was getting hot. I'm sure she couldn't miss knowing about my erection. I didn't miss knowing that she was getting hot. I could feel her heat coming right through our clothes as she pressed herself against me. I was beginning to believe that I might yet get lucky on this vacation.

Then, one of those moments happened, which I carry in my memory, like a photo in an album. I can still see it happen in my mind whenever I want to take it out and review it. I asked her if I should see her to her door. She turned her face up to look into mine. That is my favorite picture of her face.

It is perfect in its close up detail. The lighting was as soft as her smile. The desire in her eyes was only for me. This snapshot in time is etched into my memory. She looked into my eyes and into my soul; her voice was a soft, throaty whisper, as she said, "No! I want to be with you tonight. Show me where you're staying." With her head turned up to me like that, I leaned my head down and to the side to kiss her. I could see down her blouse, her nipple was as erect as my dick.

For the next few days, I had the vacation of my fantasies. I don't recall seeing any buildings. Wonderful architecture might enthrall me, but nothing has ever inspired me like the form that I had the pleasure to explore that night. We have shared more great times together, but I remember that first one with the most fondness.

There is a connection between testosterone and the ability to cerebrate, the ability to reason analytically. When a man has high levels of testosterone in his system he becomes single minded. For the last few days of my vacation I would not have been able to think my way out of a closet. I was temporarily incapacitated by a chemical overload. It might be nature's way of conserving energy or perhaps it is just that men can only support one function or heed one thought at a time. We can only work with one head at a time. When the testosterone builds up the large head seems to go comatose. When the large head starts thinking the smaller head goes dormant. It is a common observation among women, I'm told. Come to think of it; it was a woman who told me that. I wonder why I hadn't realized that before.

The last night before I was to go back to work, Annie said something that was to rock my world. It happened when Annie and I were relaxing in bed watching television, when she laughingly said, "I was very wrong with my first impression of you. You wouldn't kill anyone." I had heard her clearly enough, but I was needing a moment for the testosterone to get out of the way so that I could think and get the meaning of what she had said to sink into my realization.

I was just looking at her rather dumb-founded. She continued a little more quickly, that when she heard me say something to her in the affectation Brooklyn accent, she thought I had been sent by her ex-boyfriend's boss to find her and to kill her.

Instead of clearing things up, her explanation only confused me and bothered me more. What the hell had I gotten into? Who was this woman? Equally insistent in my brain were the questions, who the hell are her ex-boyfriend's boss, why would he want her dead, who would really do that? Then, the question came into my brain; what would he do to me if he found me here with her?

The vacation time for my brain was suddenly over. My stomach felt a little queasy with the dump of adrenalin into my system. I tried to clear my head with a deep breath. "Ok!" I told her, "Now would be a good time to let me know what is going on. What have I stepped into?"

ENTER THE HEART

CHAPTER II

YOUNG JOE

Annie began telling me her story by telling me about the people she was involved with. First there was Joe.

1933 was an uncertain year for Young Joe's family. He was too young to know that. He was the fourth child and the second son born to his parents. His parents had wanted more children, but his mother had developed diabetes during her pregnancy with him. Her doctor knew that another pregnancy could kill her. The family was Old Catholic. This meant that birth control methods were out of the question. The old doctor knew that the healthy young husband could not abstain from sex. The young woman did not like her options, but she accepted the doctor's recommendation. He did what he felt he had to do. He performed a hysterectomy and thus ensured the Joe would be the last of the young couple's children.

The family's meager economic resources were able to go a little farther through the Depression years without the extra children they had wanted. This made it possible for Joe's father to feed his family without having to go to see his great Uncle Francis and ask for a favor.

You see, Joe's family was Sicilian. They had come to America after World War I. Great Uncle Francis's family had immigrated in an earlier era. He had suffered as a teenager in New York. There never seemed to be enough. Not enough food, not enough heat in the winter, not enough air in the summer, not enough money. The good jobs weren't available to those immigrant WOPs. WOP stood for immigrants without papers. The rent for a small, vermin and bug-infested tenement was too high. The Irish clans seemed to control everything and what they didn't control, the Jews did. Even the cops were Irish. Francis learned to hate the Irish.

Some fellows in his neighborhood organized themselves to give mutual aid and protection to their fellow Sicilians. They called themselves after an old organization from the old country. They called themselves Mafia.

Uncle Francis had come a long way since then. He had moved to St. Louis to take some business there when Prohibition began. The country had been divided up. St. Louis was a plum. Francis had gotten it because he had been good at his job and he was loyal to the organization. No detail got passed him. He was good at his work, because he liked his people. He liked taking care of them, and he liked hurting people who tried to harm his people.

Francis had rules for his operation. Some rules were flexible; some were not. If you were Sicilian and you asked for a favor, you got it. Then you were indebted. You were required to return the favor. Someday, you would be expected to pay it back. Make no mistake about that, you will pay your debt.

That is what Joe's father knew. He didn't object to paying debts, but he knew that Francis would want repayment through acts, which a devout Catholic might find unethical or even immoral; to say nothing about illegal.

Joe's father had learned about electricity in Italy and how to handle electrical wires safely. He had come to America after the war had ravaged the economy in the old country. When he had arrived in America, there were already too many people on the East coast for his rural temperament. The immigration people kept trying to locate him with other Italian people. He kept telling them, that he wasn't Italian. He was Sicilian. He heard that there was more room and work in St. Louis. He discussed it with the immigration people and before long he was on his way to St. Louis.

There were job openings for electrical workers on the new phone system that was coming to St. Louis. The settlement people took him over to talk to the electrical workers union. The economy was booming. The construction industry needed people with training and experience. The language was difficult, but they saw that he could read a schematic drawing and do the work. He got the job and his family began to do well.

His wife was ecstatic. Her life had been miserable and now it had taken a decisive turn to the positive. Now they could afford to start having the babies she desperately longed for. She had hope for tomorrow.

The 1920's were good to the young family. They bought a house as soon as they had saved back enough for the down payment. The babies came a little more slowly. She was not able to deliver a child for four years. She was greatly relieved with her first child. She had begun to think of herself as being flawed, then when her hysterectomy came along she again felt flawed, but6 this was not so bad because of already having four wonderful children.

Joe's father's joy was his first son, Michael. His heart went to his two daughters. Joe's father loved him also, but he wasn't the apple of his father's eye like Michael was. Michael could do no wrong. He was not a bad older brother, but the spoiling he got from his father had its effect. Joe wasn't ignored, but he felt as though he were when he saw the special look in his father's eyes for Michael.

When the Depression hit the work slowed down to almost nothing. His father had a lot of time with no work. The parents were glad that they had been frugal during the good years and saved back some money. They didn't trust banks. They had seen what had happened to the banks and the entire economic base in the old country. Joe's father had constructed a safe out of a large electrical box, lined it with bricks and concrete, and put it into an opening in a wall in the crawl space under the house. He could access it through a loose baseboard in the bedroom closet. Inside the wall, behind the baseboard, he could reach down through the floor plate and move a brick, which gave him access to the box. He planned that thieves wouldn't find the box and it wouldn't burn up in a fire. He figured that the interest he was not getting from the bank was his insurance payment for the security.

It worked well, because when the banks did collapse, Joe's family had a nest egg. They did not have a lot, but they were able to make it without asking Uncle Francis for a favor.

Some of the younger men in Francis' organization had taken to calling him Don Francis. Francis liked the sound of that and after awhile started to encourage it among the others.

Francis encouraged the Sicilian community to socialize among themselves and to try to remain aloof from the rest of the hoi polloi. He sponsored community dances and festivals for the Holidays.

He was eager to expand his organization. He needed loyal people in his business, especially in his lieutenants. Only Sicilians could be trusted with the most sensitive tasks. Not only were they prone to be loyal, but also because they had family in the community, they had to be loyal or something unfortunate might happen to those loved ones.

Michael got drafted into the US Army just a couple months before Japan surrendered. He spent his whole duty time at Ft. Campbell, Kentucky. His father was very proud of his son. Joe noticed all of this. When Joe graduated from high school and turned eighteen he joined the Army to make his father proud of him also. That was in 1949.

The Korean War, or police action as some still call it, began in 1950 and the US Army went to war again. Joe was assigned to the 2nd Infantry Division. He saw a lot of combat and a lot of the everyday misery of the infantry soldier in Korea.

He experienced the deaths and the maiming of his companions. He learned about being scared. He felt the intense fear you have while you're waiting to have to fight for your life. He experienced how that fear evaporates as soon as the shooting and fighting starts. He became so exhausted and fatigued that he would fall asleep while standing up, leaning on his rifle, even while trying hard to stay awake.

He acquitted himself well and was promoted rapidly. He was a Sergeant, leading his squad into the battle. He kept them together and functioning as a unit during some of the worst times. His efforts saved his platoon on one occasion. Most of his men came home, thanks to his ability to lead when the pressure was on. His commander awarded him the Bronze Star. Joe just wanted to go home. When Joe returned to St. Louis, he was a different man from the boy he was when he left. His twenty-one years had weathered a major maturing experience.

His family and friends didn't know how to talk with him. They didn't know what to expect from him. His personality was quieter and much harder. They loved him, but soon they were just trying to stay out of his way. They no longer commanded his attention. They could never understand his pain, or his fear, or his new nobility. He had matured to a degree that only the combat-seasoned leader can. Only the combat experienced leader can understand it and recognize it in another man. He and his family soon acknowledged that he needed to get out of the house and into his own space.

While Joe had been in the combat theatre, the Army had held most of his wages. When he was discharged he collected a nice little bundle from those funds and the paid leave time. He wasn't sure what he wanted to do with his life, but he didn't need to get to work right away. He wanted to take a little time to sort himself out and decide what he wanted to do.

Michael had gone to work with their father. The International Brotherhood of Electrical Workers had taken him in as an apprentice when he had applied. He was now an experienced journeyman wireman and worked regular hours for good pay.

With his future looking solid, he asked his girl friend to be his wife. Of course she was happy to say yes. She had been waiting for him to ask for a couple of years, but he had waited for his apprenticeship graduation. They were in the mood to party. She became pregnant almost right away. Now she was pregnant again. They hoped the second child would be a boy. Their little girl was two when her brother was born.

Michael's wife had a girl friend over for a visit and she asked Michael to phone Joe and invite him over so they might meet. Michael phoned Joe, as requested, and asked him over for a beer and a sausage. Joe said, "No!" He didn't like being around little kids. Instead, he told Michael to meet him at Vinny's Steak House for a beer in an hour.

Vinny's had a comfortable atmosphere. It had a fireside, sports-bar environment. Autographed pictures of sports stars lined the bar wall. There was even one of Vinny having a laugh with the great legend of baseball, 'Big Jim' Dion himself. They were pictured, sitting in the very same booth, where the picture was displayed. Jim was probably the greatest baseball player to ever play the game.

Half way through their beer a cousin of theirs named Angelo saw them, came over and tried to stir up a little fun. "Hey! What's a couple of Dagos like you doing drinking beer? Don't you know Italians are supposed to drink wine? What za matta wid yous guys? You guys are going to give us a bad name. People will think you're Irish or German or something else with no class." Then he smiled broadly and continued, "Hey Mike! Hey Joe! How are you guys doing? Hey, I haven't seen you guys for – geez. How long has it been? Oh yeah! It was when Fat Tony's little girl got married. Wasn't it? Well, hey! Welcome back home Joe! Good to see you got back in one piece. Oh hey! I see my chick is trying to get my attention. That's her over there. I gotta go! Hey! I'll see you guys around"

Joe smiled at Angelo's receding back, and said, "Yeah! Good to see you too Angelo." Then he looked at Michael and said, "I don't think he took one breath in all of that." Michael laughed and said, "That has got to be the most one-sided conversation I have ever been a part of. The two brothers had a much better rapport as adults, than they ever had as children. It had been a good evening for relaxing and bonding.

The next day Don Francis knew that Joe was home and that he had matured a lot. Angelo was a good man for keeping the Don up to date on what was happening in the community. A few days later Joe got an engraved invitation in the mail. A party was being given in celebration of the Don and his wife's thirty-first wedding anniversaries. Tuxedos requested.

After he and his wife opened and acknowledged the gifts, the Don gave a slight nod to Joe and walked to the patio. Joe understood that his presence was being requested. The Don strolled towards a corner of the yard where he raised and manicured his roses. The party guests had avoided this area. Joe walked over to where the Don smelled a bloom. "Hello Uncle Francis! Congratulations to you and Aunt Elizabeth on your anniversary." In a voice strong, deep, and yet soft, the Don said, "Thank you Joseph! I have been wanting to have a minute with you. To welcome you back home and to thank you."

Joe said, "I don't understand. To thank me for what?" The Don turned about gracefully, yet with strength in his posture. He smiled, placed a hand on Joe's shoulder and said, "You well represented mankind when you put your life on the line for America, but more specifically, you did highly honor your Sicilian heritage and us, your family. We owe you a debt of honor." Joe didn't know what to say. He had never heard of anyone receiving such high praise from the Don. He managed to breathe out a, "Thank you!"

"No, No!" Interjected the Don, "It is I who thank you, and before this gets absurd, let me tell you how. I need a man of your leadership abilities for an important position in my organization. My thanks to you will be in the form of paying you handsomely to run, what will amount to being, your own business. It will be a subsidiary to my business. I will give you the direction that I want the business to go in, but the running of it is up to you. I'm sure you are up to it. Joe was stunned. He wasn't expecting this. "Can I think it over?" He asked. "Certainly!" Said the Don, "Get back to me when you're ready. Now go, and enjoy the party." Joe was glad he was living alone, because tonight he had a lot of thinking to do and he wanted some solitude to do it in.

CHAPTER III

THE GREAT JIM DION

Jim Dion was a lazy, listless kid who did not know when he was sitting on a good thing. That's the way his papa thought of him.

His papa was a fisherman. He worked himself into an early grave by just never taking an easy day. In the middle of the night he would go down to his fishing boat and get ready for another day of battling the sea. Any day he could be found, heaving on the heavy nets, and fighting to just stay on his feet and stay on the boat while the rolling and twisting deck seemed intent on dumping you over into the sea. There never was good footing. The deck was always wet with the sea and fish. There was always something to trip over. Many times when the deck tilted out from under his feet and the side rail of the boat was low on the water with nothing to hold onto, his papa would take a deep breath and turn his mind to St.

Peter and St. Anthony of Padua. Being near to a Saint is a comforting thing, especially when you are about to be awash. That's when the swell of the sea would begin to lift the boat up out of the trough. Papa would say he could feel the hands of his Saints lifting the boat up and putting it under his feet in response to his unspoken prayer. Men who live so close to death in their daily work tend to become religious or superstitious.

His papa didn't understand men, and was suspicious of them, if they didn't work hard long hours. They were pagans, if they didn't believe in god like himself and all of his fellow fishermen. His son Jim particularly distressed him; who didn't seem to care about anything.

Papa would tell the story of when he was a boy in Sicily. When his family didn't have enough of anything, he could go down to the seashore and catch a fish or two to help the family food supplies.

When the family would get tired of fish he could trade his fish at the market for some vegetables, or fruit. Some times his mama would ask him to bring home some flour so she could make the pasta or bread. When he had a good day, he could even get some eggs.

As an old man, he couldn't remember a time when he had the opportunity to just play with the other kids. His memories of his childhood were only of going to school, trying to catch fish, and going to church with his family. When he was sixteen he had an opportunity, along with some of the other young men of the island, to go to America. There was work to be had on the fishing boats in California. He was almost gleeful of the chance to go to America. He was also burdened by the sorrow of knowing that he would never see his family again. He accepted the separation stoically. After all, life isn't supposed to be fun. It's about bearing up and doing your job and your duty honorably.

The joy you get in your life comes from knowing you are doing a good job. Accept the joy you receive from your work and then you don't have to run around wasting your money and your health trying to find that, all elusive, happiness.

Jim's grandfather had taught his son, there are three reasons for not trying to find fun. One, you only have so much time. You use it for making money or wasting money. If you are looking for fun you are wasting your time. Two, you only have so much money. If you are looking for fun you are wasting your money. Third, there is the cost to your character. Instead of developing duty and honor to your family or piety to God, you are dissipating your self as a self-serving hedonist. Who has not hope for, or of, a future and no investment in those relationships, which give value, depth, and quality to life? Without these relationships, the experiences you have, which should be fun, are not enjoyable, because you are not sharing them with someone you value. The fun things and times aren't fun without the sharing. They are flat, without excitement and without satisfaction. Therefore, to spend your life looking for fun is futile. Spend your time and effort developing relationships. Work and relationships that is where the joy of life is. If you have to spend money to build a relationship, it is a no good deal. Such was the philosophy Jim's papa received from his papa. He, in turn, tried to pass it on to Jim.

When his papa arrived in America he lived aboard the fishing boat and saved every penny he could. Instead of paying for something with cash, he would try to trade work or something for what he needed. In this way, he was able to save enough, over the next half dozen years, to buy a boat of his own. It was an old wreck of a boat that everyone else was afraid of. They thought it would go down in the first storm. His papa bought it cheap.

Since he didn't have a family, he didn't waste money on a house. He put himself into the boat and into repairing it and making it sound again. By the time he married Rosa he was doing well enough to buy a little house in Martinez, California. Rosa was the daughter of a fisherman whom he had known well. They had seen each other on the docks and at the fish market for a few years.

His papa thought that the lessons and the culture he had grown up with were universal. Everybody grew up with the same experiences, the same lessons at school and the same values from church. Therefore, everyone should have the same culture, he concluded. He was quite without an understanding of his son and his values. Even though his son's life overlapped his, he didn't grow up with the same experiences or conditions at all.

Jim took some odd jobs to make a little money. He worked, although, he was not in love with work like his papa was. He wanted to get a better job and have a little more control over his own life. He felt that getting up in the middle of the night to go to work was not the kind of life he wanted. He didn't have the grades or the money for college and besides he didn't like studying. Learning was boring, and the teachers were not there to make it easy or enjoyable. He tried sales. At first, he sold newspapers. He discovered that a large bundle of newspapers were heavy to carry and you had to get up early. Work was Ok, but he wanted something where you didn't have to get up so early all the time.

He next tried selling olive oil. He had been told that sales was a good career. You don't have to labor for a dollar in your pocket. You just talk to people and then they give you money. This sounded good, but people didn't just buy. They needed to be convinced that it was something they wanted. Overcoming their reticence required a skill. You needed to convince people using logic, language, and likeableness. The only problem here was rooted in the fact that Jim, in general, just didn't like people. Of course, he also couldn't reason well against a simple, 'no' from a potential customer. In short, he had no people skills or sales ability. This sales work wasn't producing so well either.

There was a Sicilian community affairs council. They tried to coordinate the needs of the little group in the San Francisco Bay Area. When an employer, in the group, needed a job filled, they would try to coordinate the filling of the job. They liked to take care of their own. The council had been trying to find something for Jim. They sent Jim over to talk to Tony Falconi.

The casino, where Tony worked needed dealers, but the dealers had to develop a skill with their fingers and hands. They also had to develop the mental discipline to watch and remember the cards as they are played. Tony Falconi was trying to teach this skill to Jim. Jim liked the glamour and the clamor around the Casino. The appearance of easy money appealed to his weak nature.

He didn't like exercising his mind to calculate the odds on the next play or the finger and hand coordination exercises, which would make it easy to deal a particular card to a particular player at will, but he stuck with it, because of the lure of the easy money. He also liked the fact that he didn't have to get up early in the morning for this job. He began to get pretty good at the physical and mental exercises. This training would come in handy, a little later. The hand eye coordination and the ability to think ahead of the action was good preparation.

The training was coming along well, but it came to an abrupt end one night when the casino boss, Franky, wanted to see how the new dealer's training was progressing. Jim didn't make a card pass as smoothly as he should have. Franky caught it and criticized him. Jim didn't take criticism well and said something sarcastic back to Franky; who didn't take talk back from anyone, let alone a new kid. In a moment, Jim was in the alley and Tony was saying, "Good luck kid, don't come back!" As he was closing the door, Jim shouted back, "I don't need you guys. Someday, you will want me in your club." Jim's work opportunities were getting thin.

The town was forming a baseball team. Jim had played some with the local kids when he was in school and was a good athlete. Some of his friends had gone down to try out and suggested that he should do the same. Jim really didn't want to play, but they were willing to pay and he didn't have any other good work leads. He figured he would go down and just play for the few dollars they were offering until something better came along. The training he had for the casino sharpened his already good coordination, but his ability to think ahead of the play is what made him outstanding. He knew just where to take the play after fielding the ball. He appeared to be a natural at this game.

The scouts began to notice him. Opportunity came knocking and this time Jim was ready to open the door. The Pacific Coast league was a great opportunity for the young man. By the time he was twenty-two years old he was invited to try out for the New York team. The fans and the press began to talk about this new kid. His great ability and the press turned him into a sports hero. A press, ready to sell papers covering the new sports hero. Jim learned something about himself. He liked being a hero. There was just one problem. He didn't like all those people bothering him wherever he went. Why did they have to always want to talk to him? Why did they always want him to autograph something? Why did people always want something from him? Why couldn't they just idolize him and respect his privacy?

As his fame grew, other people began to take note of him and followed his playing. Jim had set new records for the game. He had helped the New York team win the World Series in 36. He was called 'Mr. Baseball'. One of the people, who was, noting what Jim was doing was Don Francis. In 1941, Jim was on a record streak when the team came to St. Louis. Don Francis went out to the ballpark to watch the game and to see this guy play in person. He loved what he saw.

While the team was showering off after the game, someone was sent in to tell Jim that he was invited to have dinner with the Don. It was an honor to be invited, but Jim was reluctant to go. There always seemed to be some fan who wanted a ball autographed or to shake hands with him. Occasionally, somebody wanted to take him to dinner. When Jim was told that the Don was a fellow Sicilian and an important man in town, he accepted the invitation.

Jim had a hunch, but just to be sure, he telephoned Tony Falconi back in Frisco. He wanted to know who this Don Francis was. Tony put the bug in Jim's ear. Don Francis was the Mafia's man in St. Louis. He is not a man to cross or insult. It is rumored that some men have disappeared for such lapses in manners.

There is the story about one successful local businessman who made some comment to an associate that he didn't like Don Francis' business. He seemed to think that some of the Don's business associates were not very acceptable in St. Louis' social circles. That man had a terrible run of bad luck and now was on the verge of bankruptcy. It was peculiar how things like that happened around the Don.

Jim met the Don at Vinny's Steak House as planned. He was surprised at how comfortable he felt with the Don. He was a very likable guy. Before long they were laughing at jokes and asking about people they might know in common. Don Francis particularly enjoyed the story of Jim's insult to Franky and his being tossed out of Franky's place.

Joining them, for a glass of wine, after the dinner, was the restaurant's owner Vinny. Jim could gather that Vinny was a respected lieutenant in the Don's operations. The camera girl came by and asked if it would be ok to take a picture. They all smiled for the camera. Jim usually tried to avoid such things. But, why not, after all, dinner had been excellent, and 'on the house'. Jim was enjoying himself. It was good, being a hero.

After the wine, Vinny excused himself. The waiter brought coffee. The Don took a more business tone to his voice. "Jim, I'm a man who does a lot business based on knowing what is probably going to happen in the future. Sometimes somebody on a sports team will need a little help. I'm glad to help out when I can. Then later on maybe that person will return the favor by telling me how the team is playing. Perhaps some key player is sick or injured. Little things like that can have a meaningful impact on the team's ability to win. Perhaps a pitcher has a sore arm or is in a slump. Things that aren't known by the public can make money for me. A little information ahead of time is good for me." Jim was getting ready to get angry.

Jim never did say he loved the game, but he never tried less than his best, ever. That would be like stepping on his own name; like, despising himself. At this moment, Jim realized what honor was, how precious it was to him, and that he did have some. Perhaps, something of his papa, had rubbed off on him.

The Don continued, "I can see that I've made you angry. That's good! I can see that you always play to win. I love that! Do you know why? Because, you're one of us. Because you are Sicilian, like me.

I only mention some of what I do, so that you will know some of the things that I do. I don't want you to be surprised if you hear or read something. I owe that to a pizano.

We don't get any respect in this country. Everybody seems to think that we are dumb, ignorant, or dirty. They try to take advantage of us at every opportunity. They want to use our backs to build their fortunes and give us nothing in return. That's not right! We are going to let them know that we aren't so dumb as to tolerate their yoke any longer. We are going to take our share and then we will put the yoke on their necks.

Do you see what I'm saying Jim? What I mean to say is this; you are a national hero and you are Sicilian. Everybody knows who you are. You are doing more for the Sicilian community in America, by being the greatest ball player in the game ever, than I can with a dozen charities.

I'm still not getting said what I want to say. Listen! You know that if I do a favor for someone, I expect them to pay back the favor. They are obligated by their honor to pay back. Now—the way I see it, you have done so much for all of us Sicilians. You have given us back our pride. We can walk around and say, "Sure! I'm a Sicilian. Just like the Great Jim Dion. We are Sicilians alike. Don't you see Jim? I, and all of us are in your debt. We owe you a favor. Jim! What can I do for you? Just name it. Anything! Anytime! Anywhere!"

Well, there it was, the offer which, when eventually accepted, would rock the world. Jim was unable to answer. He had been expecting an offer to throw a game, which he was ready to repudiate. This had caught him with a full stomach and his mind was unprepared to answer. He eventually said he didn't need a thing. The Don told him that this offer didn't have an expiration date. It was valid forever.

That night, back in his hotel bed, Jim was thinking, out loud, to himself, "Great, that's just great; now that I've done something on my own and now that I'm somebody;

now you guys want to be pals. Where were you guys before, when I needed a little help? Not only did you not help me, you threw me out of your stinking casino and told me not to come back. I told you; someday you would want me to come back. Now you guys can just fuck off. I don't need you now; so don't come around bothering me now.

Two years later, Jim got his notice from the draft board. At first, he did not believe it was a real notice. He thought it was a practical joke from some of his teammates. He was furious when it was confirmed to be genuine. He went to the team's management offices to try to pull some strings. He went to the draft board office and yelled and threatened. He was saying things like they couldn't do this to a national hero. He was the nations hope. He was Mr. Baseball. What was the nation to do while he was gone?

It crossed his mind to call in that favor from Don Francis. After he cooled down and thought about it, he decided not to do that. Don Francis was big on patriotism. He loved America and anyone who avoided the draft was a low down slime ball. Someone else had gotten that point when they had asked for his help in avoiding the draft. Jim wasn't going to do that.

He decided to stop fighting it and just go. The negative publicity, he would get from trying to avoid the draft, could hurt his hero image. Jim did like his hero image. The war would probably be over in six months, maybe a year, at the most.

"When I get back," he said told his fellow soldiers, "I'll make them pay. I won't accept no lousy first-string pay. I'm the Great Jim Dion, Mr. Baseball. I will make them pay plenty for this."

The war years were not comfortable to Jim. His teammates thought they never had it so good. While the other draftees were fighting the war, sleeping in holes in the mud, freezing in the cold, charging into hordes of enemy guns, dying by the gross, and being maimed by the score, Jim was playing baseball in Hawaii and complaining the whole time. He was so negative that his own teammates didn't hang around with him. His sour attitude was what marked him most among his fellow soldiers, not his ability.

When the war was over and he came back to New York, he was good to his word. He made them pay. The front office would not have put up with his attitude if it had been anybody else. He got away with it. He could draw the crowds. The crowds meant money. They might even win the pennant. That would mean a lot of money too. They didn't like it, but they paid. He was Mr. Baseball again. America was glad to have the war over and their hero back. Everything could return to normal again. America took Jim back into their sports headlines and into their hearts once more.

CHAPTER IV

DON FRANCIS

Jim Dion married Lynn Marie and the Sicilian community was ecstatic over the success of their favorite son. Some of the women groused that the marriage could never last, because Lynn wasn't good enough at being a housewife for a Sicilian man. They had wanted Jim to marry a Sicilian girl.

Across the country the Sicilians were feeling strong. Business had been going well for them. Now they felt like the world was their chicken; they could pluck it as they saw fit. Just like Great Jim Dion; Jim had wanted Lynn Marie and he got her. The families wanted America and they were going out to get her.

Las Vegas was a plum for Malone and Green, but there were many other cities and towns across America which most people never heard about, but these too were gems in the Mafia's crown. From Trinidad, Colorado to

Lima, Ohio. From Springfield, Massachusetts to Tampa, Florida, the country was being organized, right under the noses of the local populace. The families were busy doing favors for the local authorities and powers. They were developing business and taking control. It surprised some of the boys at how easy it was to compromise a town politician. After securing some key cities, in any given state, they went after the state politicos. After gaining the compliance of a few key people in any given state, they went after the national politicians from that state. It was the domino principle with a twist. That is a little tongue in cheek humor. You see, some times a prostitute is called a 'twist'. A community leader might be a strong anti-crime or anti-drug or anti-anything man. At a party, he would be introduced to the most beautiful woman he had ever seen. She would have a strong sexual desire for him. In no time at all you had another compromised community leader to add to your sack of marbles. Some men were more susceptible to be compromised by business contracts worth lots of money. Other men were so weak they could be compromised by fear and intimidation. It was so easy to get a community to support whatever policy you wanted. Control the press and the leaders of a community and the community is yours. Just like farming chickens, control the flock, keep the foxes out, and the eggs are all yours to take as you wish.

In St. Louis, Don Francis was expecting good things from his new lieutenant. Joe had a restaurant club and catering business. That provided the cover and some cash for the next level of business. In the back rooms were the girls. They brought in some cash, but their main job was to compromise the leading people of the town.

Every customer was photographed, from several different angles, if he was someone, who could do something for the organization, sometimes he was already bought and paid for, by his own vice. The main targets for these places were the cities' middle management people and businessmen. The person or people who controlled the police had to be compromised early in the development of the operation. Files were kept on everyone. You never knew when that customer, who was a nobody today, might be somebody tomorrow. He might be squeaky clean today, but his one time indiscretion, was photographed and would always be in the family's photo album for future use as needed. One could say, the upstairs girls opened the door to the business in the basement. There were the games. Just about anything you could ask for in the games of chance. Of course, it really isn't chance at all. That is just the impression. They are as controlled as the enforcement of the law. These games were just another layer in the business of the families. This layer, like all the others, is for developing the ways and means to get to another layer. Getting deeper and deeper into running the country as they see fit.

In a puppet show the puppet masters run several puppets and speak with many voices. In a puppet show, some of the characters seem to be fighting the efforts of others, but it is all scripted for the distraction of the audience. The puppet master determines the outcome before the first puppet takes the stage. The audience pays and the money ends up in the puppet masters pocket. That is the goal from the start. The performance is just the way to get the money from the audience. In the story of Pinocchio, a puppet becomes a living person. In real life, when a real person wants to participate as a public figure he gets entangled with a lot of strings and soon he notices that he has become a puppet. He is yanked from here to there. Someone else puts words in his mouth. He can never see exactly who is pulling those strings. He knows it only as a pressure to do this or take a stance or position there. He never really knows who the ultimate puppet master is. It is the story of Pinocchio in reverse. The tragedy of this comedy is that it is a true story. It has been going on for centuries and it will continue. Every man has some weakness. The families became experts at understanding and exploiting these human weaknesses.

Joe was the puppet master in his club. He reported to the Don who was the master of his turf. He, in turn, was answerable to others. Joe's business provided ways and means to manipulate people and power. The Don had other businesses like Joe's. Some of the Don's businesses were totally different, but they all provided a service to the Don and his organization without having to go out into the public view for these services. Early, in the development of the families' control of the states, they realized the need to own their own banks. These banking businesses provided a way to move money and people around the country to where it was needed. It was needed in various places as a string to manipulate other people with.

The vice businesses, for which the families are most famous, provide a means of getting at the resources of the public at its most primal level. Far more important though is the fact that, they provide the excuse for a large armed force, maintained by public funds, to be at the disposal of the puppet masters. To be used for enforcing the compliance, of competing interests, who might otherwise wrest control away from the families. The main competing interest is the public themselves who may want to throw off the yoke of the families.

It seems like there are always a few people in a community who are unhappy with the establishment and want to do something about it. If these people become a problem, then they are targeted to be compromised and they either take the bait or they don't. If they do go for the bait, then they are arrested and convicted. As a convicted criminal, they lose all credibility with the community and are blocked from holding public office. If they don't take the bait, then some mole would join the circle of friends of this new renegade as a supporter and report on everyone and everything that was being planned. They would then try to get the group to do something dumb. If a peaceful march or demonstration were planned, then at some inopportune moment, it would turn violent and ugly by the actions of the mole. The newspapers then would put their spin on the group and their leader. In a moment, what could have been a hero to the public becomes a crazed, antiestablishment, cult leader; bent on destroying our good standards and values. One way or another, this new natural leader becomes ineffective and subverted.

Everyone, from doughnut shop owners to bankers, from cops to mayors, was compromised by their own weaknesses. Don Francis had a lot of files and photos. It was amazing how much he got away with.

The Don's favorite game is to figure out how to get the vast sums of money, which is in private hands, under his control. The heads of the various families like to try to come up with some new scheme which will get the attention and thereby the approval of their peers. He who comes up with a great new idea is respected and venerated. As a big bonus for his efforts, he also gets all the money he has taken from the pigeons. His peers like to hear about the new scheme so that they too can get in on the action, on their turf.

Don Francis gained much respect for his insurance company scheme. It goes like this. First, start an insurance company. Sell policies to everyone. Sell at low premiums to your family and associates. Sell the same policy at high premiums to everyone else. Construct your own actuarial tables reflecting whatever demographics are there. When people ask why their premiums are high just refer them to the section, which shows that they are more likely to have a claim than someone else. If they will just stay with the program for a little while longer then their premiums will go down, if they don't have any claims that is. The preferred risk rate is just down the road a little more. Next, never pay a claim at a fair price. Always undervalue and call it depreciation. There is a great angle for avoiding paying a claim entirely if the policyholder is gullible enough. When they take out the policy, the selling agent produces a variety of possible rates depending on the buyer's insurance profile and needs. The buyer is tacitly allowed to buy a policy with a lower premium. The hook is that the buyer's profile is not quite right for the lower premium policy. He is being allowed to cheat by the tacit approval of the agent who is trying to give the impression to the client that he is helping out the client, at the expense of the company, trying to do him a good turn. This plays perfectly into the hands of the company. If the policyholder ever files a claim, the flaw in the original contract is 'discovered' by the home office and the claim is denied. If the policyholder tries to kick up a fuss, he is threatened with being taken to court on attempted fraud charges for lying on his original application. With this little ploy, you keep taking the clients money for years, with no risk of ever having to pay anything out.

If an honest insurance company comes into your territory to do business, have some of your people buy the best coverage they can afford. Then set up the accidents and the claims. Lawsuits, for big money, against the policyholders get expensive. Just bleed the new company dry. It is another source of money, which should not be ignored.

Now you have your insurance company operating. Then, the Don's Coup de Grace. All the while, the Don has been presenting himself as an upstanding citizen in the community. He contributes to political campaigns, forms a political action committee to support candidates who are 'tough on crime'. He is a real 'law and order' guy. He wants to see that his community is a good place to live and raise a family. He ends up knowing and having contacts with all the other like-minded citizens. He develops contacts on all sorts of boards and committees who like his thoughts. He knows people on the school board, on the zoning board, the commerce committee, the insurance company review board, and many other civic groups. Next, this community-oriented man thinks that for the 'public good' we ought to make it a law that everyone must have insurance. It will be a much safer state to live in. What public official can afford to argue against such influential people and argue against public safety?

What a beautiful scam! This is Don Francis' best joke on the public. The leaders of our community have influenced our politicians to make it a law that we all have to send money, through various entities controlled by the Don, into the Don's bank account. This amounts to billions of dollars every year.

If we choose not to comply, the Don, through his publicly funded forces, will deny us the right to own a car and or the privilege to drive it. If some guy, influential or not, objects to what is going on, an attempt is made to compromise him. If the guy won't be compromised, then there is the whole continuum of threats and force, which can and will be applied, up to and including, until death do us part.

One of the sweet parts of taking your operation 'legal' is that the public pays for the Don's soldiers. The Don does have some private 'soldiers' he can use when he has too, but he prefers to use the ones we pay for. The police! These public servants, serve the law and their commanders, who take their orders from the people in office, who in turn take their directions from the people to whom they owe favors, who is our man, the Don. The laws are written in a convoluted way on purpose. They can be interpreted, to the benefit of the person with the most influence. It is generally suggested to the lawmakers that we need such a law for the public good and to maintain law and order. So, the police end up controlling the public; sometimes against the publics own best interests, because 'it's the law'. Who can argue against the law? Having law is a good thing. We cannot have a civilization without laws. We cannot pick and choose which laws we will or will not obey. The laws are written by our representatives, whom we elected into office, therefore they are the laws, which reflect the will of the majority of the people. Etc., etc.

Ahhh! The righteous indignation of the enforcers of the Don's will. Interestingly enough, the majority of the laws and their enforcement are good. Nobody wants a lawless society; especially people like Don Francis. He and we want a socially responsive community for all the civilized people to live in. It is the very best environment for his kind of business to flourish in. Other crime would be competition. He wouldn't like that.

The Don doesn't care about the mundane pedantic running of society. The elected and hired servants will take care of that. It's only the occasional law, which needs to be passed, or the favor that needs to be addressed.

The old puppet master likes to rehearse his puppets so that their strings don't get crossed up. If that were to happen, some puppet might move to someone else's will. That would not be in the plan. If a puppet's strings got tangled up too badly, they might have to be cut.

The Irish orders had learned the same lessons that the Sicilians had. They and other immigrant groups that had their loyal order of, or their fraternal and paternal order of, or their protective society of. As immigrants, they all had been preyed upon by the unscrupulous elements in our society. By forming their societies, they were able to provide some relief for their people. The Kelly family formed a family Mob within the Irish protective order.

Some of the Irish groups became more than just protective brotherhoods. They became the Mob. They liked being tough and it was a short, easy step to becoming a bully. Protecting the families became protecting the gang. Protecting the neighborhood became protecting our turf. Protecting the rights of our people became protecting our business interests. The businesses, which, had been set up to help the people of the neighborhood, became business to benefit the Mob.

There was little difference between the Sicilian Mafia and the Irish Mob. They competed for the same reasons, the same turf, and the same market. In some towns the different gangs had different neighborhoods and more or less kept the peace between themselves with only a few notable exceptions.

The peace was generally kept, because of the skill or ruthlessness and reputation of one or two men in each organization. Over the years, even in times of peace, the two organizations kept wary eyes on the activities of the other. Sean Kelley was determined to rise to the top of his organization and then to control the country. To do that, he needed a peace between the Mob and the Mafia

CHAPTER V

GUNNER MIKE

M ike Beninni grew up in a little town in Ohio. His parents were killed in their car while trying to cross a railroad one night. It was a rainy night and the crossing didn't have any warning lights in those days. Mike survived the crash, because he had been asleep on the back seat of the car. The train cut the front half of the car off like it had been cut off with a large shear. Mike was nine years old at the time.

Born in 1920, Mike was an only child. His parents spoiled him in spite of his father's persistent claim that, "No son of mine is going to be soft." Mike's Aunt Mary, his father's sister, took him into her home to rear. Her husband had died one year earlier from complications, after an earlier stroke. She was fifty- four years old, in good health and a little lonely in her house. She had five grown children, who were raising families of their own.

Aunt Mary had a farm of eighty acres, which she leased to a neighboring farmer. She still lived in the farmhouse and kept a few chickens and pigs in the barn. She seemed to be the most content when she was in her garden. She loved growing things. She kept her house clean and picked up at all times. The only time there was ever any mess, was when she was preparing something in the kitchen, and it seemed like she was always making something. The kitchen was always cleaned up right after.

Aunt Mary had an annual schedule she followed. She was always busy at something. In the spring, she was getting her garden 'starts' together in the kitchen, so that as soon as the ground was ready she could get into her garden. In the summer, she had sweet corn to husk or peas to shuck, pickles or tomatoes to can. In the autumn, she was baking either bread, or pies or cookies for the upcoming Holidays. Then, there was the sausage to make. That was always after the first hard freeze of the season. The neighbor, who rented the plow land, came over and did the butchering for her. He and his family made a kind of a festival of it. In the winter, she decorated the house for the Holidays and made all kinds of ornaments to be put up and around.

The rest of the house was always the same tidy, always ready for guests, place. There was never anything out of place. It was like a static display in a museum. The only time she was in there, other than those times when she did have guests, was when she was in there to dust or vacuum, which she did every Wednesday. The kitchen was the real living room, because that is where she lived her life. This room was always in a state of flux. It was a very dynamic center of activity. You could say it was the heart of the home, because it seemed to have a pulse. With Mary's calm spirit and happy heart, it was a good home for Mike to grow up in.

After the death of his parents, Mike became a quiet boy who kept his thoughts to himself. He got along well with his aunt and seemed to enjoy helping her with anything she was doing. Whether it was making up the bed, baking bread, painting the gutters, chopping wood, gardening, or butchering a chicken for dinner, Mike did it all to the best of his abilities.

Mike became a person who enjoyed doing a tough job well. Carrying buckets of water to the chickens and pigs and gardening, along with the other chores, began to toughen his body. When he was thirteen he started cutting down trees with the neighbor, who rented the farm. There was a wooded part of the farm, from where they got their winter firewood. Mike began to develop stamina by swinging an axe and drawing a crosscut saw. When he was fourteen, Aunt Mary showed him how to use the twenty two-caliber rifle. Her husband had bought it for shooting squirrels for stew.

There was a large ditch bisecting the farm. It ran straight for a few hundred yards before turning to follow the land's contour. It was an excellent place to learn and to practice shooting. The bullet was always backstopped in the ditch bank. Mike had excellent eye- sight and coordination. Plinking at tin cans one hundred yards away became too easy. Brightly colored pop bottle caps became his favorite targets. He was hitting the one-inch targets almost every time.

When he was fifteen, Mike started to grow to be bigger than his peers. Aunt Mary thought he could handle something bigger now. A day before pheasant season opened, Aunt Mary called Mike to the kitchen. Out from a tall cabinet, by the door, she removed a twelve-gauge shotgun. She told him, he was big enough to handle the large gun now. She showed him the gun's action and how to stand strong when you shoot it, so you can absorb the recoil comfortably. She explained how to lead the rabbit or pheasant and for the meat's sake, don't shoot too soon. Control your startle reflex, let the gun sight come to bear on the prey, while the prey is moving away, you are synchronizing the muzzle's swing to the prey's movement. You then pass the prey with the muzzle and at the right moment squeeze the trigger. With a little practice, you will know the amount of lead necessary for the distance and the speed of the prey.

Mike's first pheasant kill ended up being just a cloud of feathers, blood and bits. Now he understood what it was like to be startled by a flushing pheasant and to shoot too soon. He developed the ability to control every movement, in spite of the startle, and to coldly calculate the placement of the shot on the rapidly moving target.

More than once, when Mike was hunting with a neighbor or a school chum; a rabbit or a pheasant would flush and the other shooter would fire and miss, and fire and miss again. All the while, Mike would be sighting and following the target; waiting for the shooter to give up. Then, as the prey was becoming more distant, they might exclaim that the prey was too far away now. That is what Mike was waiting for. He would fire his only shot and drop the animal. Then he would smile a little and say, "No! It isn't too far away yet." He enjoyed shooting and the admiration of his fellow hunters was the trophy he enjoyed the most.

In high school, Mike ran for the track and field team. He enjoyed the competition and the fact that he could compete as an individual. It wasn't that he didn't like team sports. It was that he would demand the same effort and intensity out of his teammates. He didn't like to put forth every bit of effort he could and lose, because someone else on the team had let down. In track and field, you won or lost on your own effort.

Martha Lazzaro was the girl Mike was in love with in high school. She had the whole six-pack. She was a pretty girl. She was always well groomed. She had a smile for everyone. She had a great looking body. She was smart. Her family was successful in the community. A guy couldn't want more.

It was in their freshman year, at a sock hop dance after a football game, that they shared each other's first real kiss. Neither of them was allowed to date yet, but the dances, at school after the games, were allowed. They were both pretty shy. Martha liked Mike more than any boy she had ever known. They made it a point to find each other at each of the dances.

In their sophomore year, they shared the sock hops and going for a soda with friends. In their junior year, Mike had a driver's license and was allowed to borrow Aunt Mary's model A Ford. He would wash it and polish it up every week. He and Martha could now spend a little time alone together. Martha made it very clear, that it was enjoyable to snuggle and kiss, but she wanted to save herself for her honeymoon. Mike and Martha were most alive when they were in each other's company.

Their senior year was a year of devastation. Martha had started dating one of the football players. Bill O'Conner's dad had a retail business in town. He drove a big Buick, which Bill could take his dates home in. At the sock hop, after the game, Mike asked Martha about it. She explained that her parents thought it would be better if she dated some other boys while she was yet young, and met other young men before settling down and marrying. Mike could feel his gut go tight with disappointment, but he couldn't argue against her parent's wishes.

The Senior Prom, in the spring, entered his mind. Mike said he realized that it was months away yet, but that he had always wanted to take only her. He asked her to not go with anyone, but him. She quickly reassured him. "Of course we will go to the Prom together. You're still my best friend." Those words were supposed to have been comforting, but to Mike they cut into his heart like a knife. Mike had always wanted to be her only boyfriend, now he was hearing that he was just, a friend. Best friend, was only a qualification for a friend and not in the same romantic position at all. Mike thought he could feel his head ache with the sound of that pronouncement.

His real suffering started about Christmas time when Martha began to get distant and reticent around Mike. She didn't enjoy dancing at the sock hops and she didn't smile so much any more. Shortly, she started avoiding the sock hops completely.

In February, Mike wanted to talk to Martha about coordinating their Prom plans. She wasn't in her classes. Her girl friends had not seen her for a few days.

Mike called her on the telephone. It was Martha's mother who answered. She had always liked Mike and she tried to choose her words carefully. She was picking her words and her way through a difficult situation like a person walking through a cactus patch.

Martha was pregnant! She wouldn't be going with anyone. She was withdrawing from school. Her family didn't want any flap. Bill O'Conner was no help and even disclaimed being the father. He had even suggested that the baby was Mike's. Martha had been dancing with Bill, at the sock hop after the last game of the season. Some of the other players wanted to sneak out, to go and drink some beer to celebrate the end of the football season. They were going to meet, at an old quarry outside of town, to have a private party. Martha was aware that there would be beer at the party, but she decided to go along anyway.

After the party, Bill wanted to sit in the car and kiss. Martha said ok. Some of the other couples sat in their cars and snuggled. After a little while, everyone was gone. Then he began to touch her breasts. She objected, because she didn't think this was the right thing to do yet in her life. Her persisted and she did like the feeling in her breast, so she allowed him to open her blouse and brassiere. It did feel good and she was feeling a little unbalanced from the one beer, she had allowed herself to be talked into drinking. Then she felt Bill's hand moving up her leg, towards her panties, towards her crotch, towards her pussy. She had not thought that he would try to do this until after she was ready and they had talked it over, but there was his hand, without her permission, coming to snatch her cherry.

She grabbed at his hand to stay it and broke off the kiss to tell him no. Emphatically, no! She would not allow this to go on. He was violating her trust in him. Bill had drunk two beers. More than he had ever drunk before. He was feeling very aroused sexually after experiencing her breasts. He wanted more and he considered her to be his. She was just trying to keep up an image, by saying no. She really wanted him to be a man and do this to her, he thought. He never even considered that she was really, horrified by his actions. He was so much stronger than she was. Her efforts to push him away were to no effect. She tried to scream for help, but they were alone at the quarry, two miles from anywhere.

After he was done, she was berating him for raping her. He told her it was her fault for leading him on that way, making him think that she wanted him to fuck her. If she had not wanted to fuck, why had she let him touch her breasts and why had she kissed him so passionately? He continued to tell her, that if she even tried to accuse him of rape he would tell how she left the dance and came willingly with him to the quarry to drink beer and party. He would tell how she started kissing on him and how she took off her blouse and bra for him to ogle her body. There were other kids at the party who could confirm that she had gone to the party and drank beer.

She was really angered at how he distorted the facts. She was also angry with herself for allowing herself to get into the position where he could lie and people would believe him and not her. She was also shattered by her own self-image. She had let her self down. She had truly wanted, more than anything, to be a good girl and to save her self for her honeymoon. Now she felt ruined.

She thought of Mike. She longed to be in his arms now and to just be comforted by him. He was the one she truly loved. She had wanted Mike to be her husband, to be her first, to share each other's first sexual explorations. It was supposed to have been something meaningful, something romantic. Not some fight and rape like dumb animals. She was sick to her stomach and vomited. She thought of what she had done to Mike and their relationship. She wished that she were dead. She wanted to see Mike again. She wanted to embrace him. She wanted to explain the truth to him. She felt so guilty at having let him down that she couldn't bring herself to face him.

A month later and her menstrual cycle was two weeks over due. She was feeling very worried. She began feeling sick to her stomach in the mornings. She knew what it meant. She felt that fate had raped her also. She sobbed and cried out to God, to let her die. Her mom came to her room when she heard the crying. They talked it out. She had kept the rape a secret for fear of her reputation and the nagging worry that it had been her fault. Her mom took her to the doctor and in a week she knew the horrible thought was a fact. She was pregnant.

Martha was going to be sent to live with an aunt in Cleveland. There, she would have the baby and put it up for adoption. She would get her high school G.E.D. and start a new life somewhere else. Any place where her mistake would not be known.

While Mrs. Lazzaro was talking, Mike was changing in his inner person. By the time he hung up the phone, he was a different person. He was now maleficent. He had the kind of evil anger that comes from pure hate —newly born. He was walking around in a daze and rehearsing something in his mind, "assume a strong, on balance, stance. Don't let the startle reflex ruin your shot. Control your breathing while bringing the gun to bear upon the target. Align the sights on the animal." In his mind's eye, the animal in the sights was Bill O'Conner.

Something was pulling on him. He realized it was Aunt Mary. She was asking him what was going on. He noticed then that he already had the shotgun on his arm and a box of shells in his hand. He was readying to load the gun. Aunt Mary got the information out of him about Martha.

Her tactic was not to tell him no. She knew this young man and she had seen this look before on other men's faces. She just told him to wait for Uncle Benny to come over to help him. The tactic worked, because he agreed to wait for Uncle Benny, but only if he was coming over right now.

Aunt Mary got on the phone, but Mr. Muma, from the farm down the road was on the party line. There were four farmhouses on the same line. Aunt Mary told Mrs. Muma to ring her back when she was done talking so that her call could be made. The ladies on the line were always polite and friendly to each other.

Then Aunt Mary took the shotgun shells from Mike explaining that they weren't the right kind for his purposes. Rabbit and pheasant shot was too light for skunks she said. It also got the situation controlled until Uncle Benny could get there. She put the shells in the silverware drawer when Mike wasn't looking. In a few minutes the phone rang. It was Mrs. Muma telling her, the line was free now.

CHAPTER VI

UNCLE BENNY

Uncle Benny was from Gary, Indiana. He had grown up running around Chicago doing odd jobs for the organization. When Capone came to Chicago he brought his ruthless ways with him. He quickly moved into the boss' position and stayed there for a long time. When Capone took over the business organization he inherited Benny. Capone's style of business was a lot more aggressive than his predecessor 's. Soon there was a lot more shooting going on in town. Some of the guys just carried a gun without taking the time to really get to know it well, or study how it worked, or to develop a fine skill with it. A few of the men put in some practice time and did learn how to make the piece, as if it were, an extension of their arm. Uncle Benny was an expert with his guns. He particularly liked the Thompson, 45 caliber and sub-machine gun. It was a lot of fun to shoot and one

Ben Romen

of the things Benny liked about the 'Tommy Gun' was the fact that when you pulled it out to shoot, the other guys didn't stand their ground and shoot back. They just scattered like rats.

His next favorite piece was the sawed off, double barreled, 12 gauge, shotgun. It was fast into action, because you didn't have to take the time to aim it. Just point and pull. It was only a fraction of a second faster than a handgun, but that fraction of a second gave you the first shot and the first shot from the 'Street Sweeper' usually allowed you to seize control of the shoot out.

There are usually two kinds of guys on your target. The first kind will react by first trying to get his gun out, pointed in your direction, and firing before thinking about getting behind cover. The other kind of guy tries first to get out of sight before going for his gun. The first kind of guy is usually the more aggressive type of shooter, but he is also the first to die on his shadow. If you were to back out of the place, right after the first volley of shots and sped away, you would have dealt a terrific blow against your adversary. Half of the adversary's men will be dead and it will be the more aggressive half at that.

Let's say that you have a particular target, who is surrounded by other shooters. The first two guys into the place will be the 'street sweeper' and the 'Tommy gun'. They will take out the aggressive guys at the door opening. The Tommy gun will keep everybody under cover while the hand gunners go in to take aimed shots, at close range, at anyone foolish or brave enough to try to see around a corner and do anything. They also 'finished off' anyone who was already down, but alive, and could shoot at your back. Behind these guys came the 'hit man'. He was the

- 57 -

guy who knew the particular target on sight. His job was to move, with this fusillade, into and through the target area. He was looking for, and saving his ammunition for, the specific target. A lot of these guys carried two guns. One was for their moving protection while the other was kept in reserve for the specific target. You never wanted to fight your way into the hive, to finally confront the target, with an empty piece.

Benny liked all the action. It gave him an adrenalin rush better than sex. That was his favorite aphrodisiac. His best nights were when he had to go out on a shoot out and then he would go home, to his woman and have the best sex. Benny was good at being the 'hit man', because he could hold his mud. He had the courage to walk through the shooting, going on all around him, and look for the specific target.

He liked to carry a Colt, 45 caliber, 6 shot revolver for the hit, and a Colt, 45 caliber, model 1911, semi-automatic, with extra magazines, for walking around. He liked the combination of the reliability of the revolver and the firepower of the semi-auto. Benny's signature hit was three rounds, one in the chest between the nipples, one in the mouth, and one through the ears. Benny had been surprised once, by a guy living, after Benny had left him for dead. He wasn't going to let that happen again. Somebody once asked Benny about the message that he might be sending with this kind of a hit. Benny told him, that the message was that he was dead. There isn't going to be any aspirin in the morning to make the headache better.

Aunt Mary and Uncle Benny were related somehow, but it was from back in the old country and nobody seemed to know just how anymore.

Uncle Benny was in Lima visiting some old friends and recuperating. He had taken a bullet a few months earlier. He had been taken to Trinidad, to have the doctor take out the bullet and reconstruct the leg, as well as he could. After a couple of months in the underground hospital he was fit enough to recuperate with family care.

Mary was on the phone, telling him that she was fixing his favorite meal, spaghetti with apple pie for dessert. He should come out to the farm and share some with her and Mike.

Uncle Benny got one of the Guagentti boys to drive him out to the farm. He could tell from the message that it was a family business matter and that it involved Mike. He was glad for a reason to get out of the house. He was getting better a getting around with a cane. He was hoping that the leg would heal well enough to allow him to drive again someday.

At the farm, Mary did indeed have a spaghetti dinner and an apple pie ready. She had always been distant from the family's business, but she was nobody's fool. She was shrewd enough to know that if she had said, on the public phone, that they were having spaghetti and apple pie, they were most definitely going to have spaghetti and apple pie. It was no good, to have a coded message, if some outside observer could see right through it.

After learning about the situation, Uncle Benny took charge. He did not tell Mike, "No!" He just said, "Not now! Not here!" He told Mike that he would need more training before going out and whacking a guy. It may need to be done, and the guy deserved it, but if you do it wrong, you could end up dead or in jail and that ain't good.

First, you gotta develop some skill with guns. What you have, from hunting, is a good start. This man-shooting thing is different. The guns are different, to begin with. Men don't always act the same as rabbits when you point a gun at them. They will try to shoot back, if they have a gun, and that makes it a whole different kind of game. And then there are the cops. We will have to put them into the plan. They will try to put you away for doing, what it is that, you have to do. This guy, O'Conner, who is he? More to the point, who is his family? Mike didn't know the answers to Uncle Benny's questions and he didn't care. He just wanted to make Bill O'Conner suffer for what he had done to Martha and to him.

Uncle Benny took him to the woods, everyday that the weather was good, to practice with the handguns. It was easy to find out that Bill's family was not connected. Uncle Benny educated Mike about the workings of the organization while they practiced. He explained to Mike how the Irish gangs were such a pain in the ass to the Sicilian families. Every time you turned around there was an Irishman, wanting to take over your territory. It seemed like you couldn't open a bottle of whiskey without seeing a Kelly or a Kennedy or an O'Bannon. "You'll see, Mike, one day they will push too far and then they'll have to be taken out. Right now, this guy O'Bannon, in Chicago, is becoming a real pain in the ass. Al is not going to put up with his crap much longer. I know Al. I can feel it coming." This, Uncle Benny told Mike in February 1937.

Uncle Benny also leveled with Mike on his obligation to the family. "We will set up an alibi for you so that people will see you some place else when it's time. We will supply a car and somebody who can drive it. I'll be with you for back up and to see that nobody else gets involved. For this favor, we don't want nothing. It's just that someday, we will ask you to return the favor and we will expect you to do it; whatever it is Mike. Understand this! When we ask you to pay back your favor, you are obligated to do so. Don't even think about not doing what we ask of you. Capice? Do you understand Mike? Ok! Are you sure you want to do this thing? Ok! Now look! Now that we are going to do this thing together; now it is our thing. La Cosa Nostra! Understand? Good! So! I think you're ready. When do you want to do it?

On March 1, at precisely six P.M. Two young men got into an altercation in a respectable hotel restaurant in Toledo. One man quickly slugged the other on the eye. The victim of the attack immediately put his hand over his eye and thereby obscured his face. His physical description was the same as Mike's. The waiter immediately intervened, settling the dispute, with apologies to the restaurant patrons, and escorted the injured young man to the kitchen for first aid. Both the waiter and the assailant were prepared to swear in court that the man who took the hit was Mike. They were the only two people who would have seen the victim's face clearly. The other patrons would believe it was Mike, because they didn't get a good look at his face, what with the hand over his eye that way and besides, he was wearing Mike's suit. It is amazing how eyewitnesses will see, just what you want them to see. After Mike's business was done, but before they returned home, Uncle Benny would place a pool ball inside of a handkerchief, place it against Mike's cheekbone, beside his eye. He then took a second pool ball and struck the first one a sound rap. The result was a nice shiner, which Mike would say he just got in Toledo.

In fact, Mike was sitting beside Uncle Benny in the rear seat of a new Cadillac. Tony, 'The Wheel' liked Cadillacs and this black one had caught his eye a month earlier. He followed it around for a few days to learn where and when it was parked. A doctor, who worked at the General Hospital, in Cincinnati, owned it. At night, it was parked in a garage, in a suburb of Cincinnati. In the day, it was parked at the hospital. The doctor, an older gentleman, came to work early at five A.M. There were not many people around at that hour. Tony pinched the car right after the old man went into the hospital. Tony had the time to do his work with the minimum possibility of being seen.

He had several hours to retune the engine, increase and balance the air pressure in the tires, and fuel up the tank. He dropped a couple of 'moth balls' into the fuel tank. The naphthalene would cause the fuel to burn hotter and faster. They will ruin an engine after awhile, but for the time being, it will run like a rabbit. Tony didn't care if he took ten years off the life of the engine. He wouldn't be driving it for very long anyway. For that little while, it would outrun any police car.

Mike was surprised at himself for being so scared. His flush of hate had subsided. He was still angry and when he had given the situation more thought he still came to the conclusion that William O'Conner needed to die. If he had only insulted Mike, he could have been forgiven, but he had ruined Martha's life. For that, he needed to pay with his life.

When he felt his determination waning, all Mike needed to do was to think about what he and Martha had lost to this Irish pig and his anger would boil again. Mike decided that what he had heard about the Irish must be true. They only wanted what was yours, for their own amusement, to be discarded when they were done with it.

"Careful Mike," Uncle Benny was saying, "If you squeeze that rod any tighter, you might break it." Mike had chosen, and was holding the 45, six shot revolver. It was more reliable and its longer barrel would make it easier to point accurately in the rush of the moment. They were waiting in the car. It was parked on the curb beside the park. The park had a large hedge of bushes along the sidewalk. On the park side of the hedge was a stand of trees, several of which were evergreens. Bill traveled this route, through the trees in the park, to and from school. This was a short cut for some of the school kids. Bill played basketball and the team practiced after school. After he showered, Bill would head home through this park at about six o'clock every evening. At this time of year, in northern Ohio, it was dark and cold at this hour and most people were home eating dinner or otherwise indoors.

Mike was wearing some boots, a large hat, and a huge overcoat that Uncle Benny had bought from a second hand store in Dayton for this occasion. They would be discarded in some other town later that same night. After sitting there for a while, Uncle Benny nudged him. Mike had been looking at the gun in his hands. "Is that him?" Uncle Benny asked.

Coming across the park was Bill. He was walking fast. Mike's legs seemed unable to move. Uncle Benny laid one hand on top of the gun and leaned across Mike to unlatch the door. Then he said, "Martha needs your help in doing this. Make it right for her." He then nodded toward the open door. Mike found his feet moving. It was like his mind wasn't there. He could see himself moving, but he wasn't causing his body to move. It was like he was sitting in a theater watching the action happening on the screen. He wasn't doing it. He was only watching it happen. It was almost, an out of body experience, but from within his body, from somewhere behind his eyes, looking out through them. He was watching his body go through the hedge and towards Bill. He wasn't directing it. It was going of its own will. He was partly horrified by what he was seeing his body do, yet he didn't try to stop it.

He knew that it had been decided and now there was no stopping this runaway action. He saw the distance close. He saw Bill look up at him, not recognizing him at first, then the look of confusion, then the look of recognition, now a look of anger. There is the gun coming up out of the bottom of the picture. Bill's face turns to stark terror, then to a pain filled grimace as the gun recoils, the muzzle flipping up again and again. Now, Bill is lurching, falling backwards and down, his legs flailing the air like he is trying to run. The gun muzzle keeps flipping up. His eyes, wider now than they have ever been, are looking back now, right into Mike's eyes. Mike can see Bill scream a choked primal scream of death, but Mike doesn't hear it. Mike doesn't hear the gun exploding the air with pressure waves. He feels himself shouting something and he barely hears himself. "Why?" "You son of an Irish whore." "Why?" "Why did you have to fuck over Martha?" "She was mine, you bastard." "Now, die! You fuck! Die! Go to hell and rot you bastard."

Mike felt himself coming back into control of his own body. Bill was almost still and still looking at him. Bill began to try to crawl away. Mike didn't know how many bullets he had fired. He pointed the gun carefully, from a foot away, at the staring eye, and this time deliberately pulled the trigger and shouted, "Quit looking at me you bastard. You did this to yourself. Now go to hell!" The gun recoiled, and Mike pointed it again at the mass that had been a head. He pulled the trigger again and nothing happened. He had expended all of his ammunition. He lowered the gun and looked at the body. It wasn't moving at all now. There was blood everywhere.

The rage drained out of him leaving him feeling weak. Panic began to fill him, "What have I done? Oh God! Now my life is done, I'm a murderer. The cops will be after me. They'll fry me in the chair. God! What will I do? Where will I go?

He heard somebody behind him whistle. He turned and saw Uncle Benny. He was swinging his arm, and saying, "Ok! Come on! Let's go! Hurry up! People will be coming. You don't want to be here when they get here. Come on!"

Mike started to move. At first his legs didn't want to move, but they got the hang of it and pretty quickly he was running to the car. Uncle Benny held the door while

Mike jumped in. Uncle Benny looked at a car parked a block away and nodded. Then he piled in and Tony drove away very smoothly and at the speed limit, never exceeding it. From the first shot until they were moving down the street was about one minute.

The car that had been parked a block away sped over and stopped where the Cadillac had been parked. A man and a woman got out and went over to the body. They shouted at the body, "Hey buddy are you Ok? Are you hurt bad?" They also pulled on his coat and opened it up to check his wounds. Then other people started to show up from the houses near by. The first couple, in their apparent attempt to help the victim, walked all around the area of the body. In a minute, the ground around the body was a mess with many new footprints. Any old prints were now totally unrecognizable as such. In a little while, the police sirens could be heard. The couple shuffled back to their car to wait there. Tony had the Cadillac five miles away before the police arrived at the scene.

The witnesses said that they saw what looked like a robbery or a drug deal gone bad. They thought that the car was a green Chevrolet. They both agreed that the man they saw was short, stocky, and middle aged. They both thought that they might be able to recognize him, if they ever saw him again. Yes! He had been alone.

The police didn't have much to follow up on. The good Samaritans had destroyed the whole crime scene. With the victim's coat opened like that, it could have been a robbery gone wrong. His wallet was missing. The couple had not only destroyed the scene around the body, but they had even destroyed any footprint evidence where the perpetrator had walked, by walking in the same path.

They even managed to contaminate the car's parking spot. In their enthusiasm to help, they had totally destroyed the entire scene. At least they got a good description of the killer and his car. The police were confident that an all points bulletin would snag him up. They would soon have their suspect; they were confident.

After the police were done questioning the helpful couple, they were free to go home. Sam and Leona then drove back to Cleveland. They had just earned twenty dollars each for tonight's work. If there was anything in the boy's wallet, they could keep that as a bonus.

In their investigation, the police learned about Mike's anger at Bill. They questioned him. The black eye was a very colorful thing by then. His alibi was sound. The police had only talked to him, because they were trying to be thorough. They were talking to everyone who had known the victim or had ever had contact with him. Martha had been in her Aunt's custody in Cleveland when the crime had happened. They never talked with her. After all, they knew what the killer looked like. He was a short, stocky, middle-aged man probably a transient. After awhile the police were busy looking into new problems and the murder of Bill O'Conner just faded into the past.

Aunt Mary pushed Mike back into school. He didn't object, but he almost failed out. He just didn't care about trying anymore. He did manage to pass his exams and graduate. Mike didn't have any plans to do anything, now that Martha was gone. He was completely dispirited.

Uncle Benny had come back to Lima to see Mike graduate. After seeing Mike's situation, Uncle Benny advised Mike to volunteer for the draft. To get your military draft obligation out of the way and to see and experience something different from Lima. "When you get out of the service we'll talk. I'm sure we'll be able to find something good for you to do."

The Marine Corps was glad to have Mike. For the first several months Mike didn't have to think. Just do what you're told. The regimented life and the physical demands were great therapy. And nobody wanted to know how you felt about anything or what you were thinking. Mike thrived.

ENTER THE HEART

CHAPTER VII

HELLO AGAIN

The new drilling platform was taking shape and we were even a little ahead of schedule. I was thinking that now would be a good time to take a short vacation. The North Sea is going to go into its usual foul weather cycle in October. When that happens, we start losing time on our construction schedule. Then the bosses are loath to approve vacation time. September usually isn't bad, but the seas are starting to get rougher and there is always the possibility of an early storm. The weather in August is usually the best for supplying the platform, for the coming winter. Everything from welding rods to beer and socks. Like I said, it's a good time to take a couple of weeks and disappear or as I call it, vacation.

A year ago, I had planned to visit Paris at this time. Since I met Annie, last February, I cannot stop thinking that Italy has a lot of wonderful sights I haven't seen yet. Annie and I had been writing to each other and we thought we could coordinate a couple of weeks in Florence. She thought I would enjoy the sight seeing around that fine old city. I was also thinking it would be nice to see Annie, in the flesh again. I had been seeing her in my mind for the last several months. As nice as that was, it wasn't helping me to sleep. I was eager to be in her company again. My eyes wanted to see her again, my ears wanted to hear her voice again, my arms wanted to hold her close again, as for the rest of me; let's just say, it was looking forward—to her again also.

Beyond that, I was caught up in her story. She had begun, when we were in Milan, to tell me about some of the people involved in the story, but we had run out of time and I had to leave before finding out what it was all about and just who was her boy-friend and his boss. Was he really ready to kill her? What could she have seen or know that would warrant killing her? What would they do to me if they knew that I was now her man? Yeah! I wanted to know more of her story, but there were other, more pressing, desires we needed to take care of first. We could wait until the second day to get back to her story, maybe even the third day.

Florence was a good suggestion of Annie's. The old church buildings are marvelous. The city is full of wonderful architecture that draws your attention and invites your eyes to linger and study to appreciate the lines of force as they are routed so inspiringly through the structure. The blending of the functionality of a building with the art of flowing lines and proportionate balance was mastered by some of the men who built Florence.

I look at what we build today when the dictates are to minimize costs and maximize commercial space and I feel that man, who once was so noble as to build beauty and grace into his structures, has moved to the modern approach. This approach is one of just being a purveyor of building space and men who design this way are just common merchants.

When I visit the places in the world, where man has built something grand, I look upon them and my spirit is enthralled. From the Sphinx of Egypt to Angkor Wat of the Khmer Cambodians and from Tijuanaco in South America to Notre Dame in Paris, we can see clearly that it is within man's nature, from ancient times, to create marvels. We can do this when we allow our spirits to cooperate and when we determine that we will do so.

We can also see that when we let selfish greed lead we don't create, we just build. We build to enhance individual financial wealth and ignore our need for spiritual wealth, and our culture is stifled. An old city is the remains of a culture, which has passed away. We can tell a lot about its citizens by what is still there. Were they passionate? Were they religious? Were they wealthy, educated, and graceful? Did they love art? Were they hedonists? Were they engineers? Did they think about the meaning of life or simply live for the moment? These clues to a past culture tell us more about the minds, the motives, and the feelings of the people than their own skeletons. Yes! Studying an old city's architecture is like exploring a past people, and I find it enjoyable.

As Annie and I toured the city, I explained about what I was looking at and why. She began to develop an appreciation of my hobby and I began to appreciate the fact that Annie was not only sexy; she was smart. She didn't have much formal education, but her ability to learn and understand was wonderful. I was having fun, seeing that she was enjoying learning about these things, which I enjoyed. That is when it began to dawn on me; I was starting to fall hard for this woman. I could feel that she was falling for me too. I wasn't sure that I wanted that to happen. I still hadn't resolved a lot of important issues surrounding her.

That night, after dinner, we shared a bottle of wine. I waited until after the first glass to tell her I wanted to know about her ex-boyfriend and his boss. She had told me a lot, but nothing about him. It was time that I knew who he was.

She told me his name was Leo. His boss was Joseph, called Young Joe. There were so many Joes in the family that they all had a nickname to differentiate them. There was Old Joe, Big Joe, Little Joe, Sunny Joe, Mean Joe, etc. and there was Annie's acquaintance Young Joe.

He was from St. Louis. He was an organization man, which is to say, Mafia. His boss was Don Francis. Don Francis had sent him to New York to open a restaurant club. Young Joe had owned a business in St. Louis for years and now the Don wanted him to open a new business in New York. The real reason Don Francis sent him to New York was so that he could have an eye and an ear in New York. What are the New York families doing? You never knew when some up and coming wise guy might get the idea that he could run somebody's business better and would try to take over their turf. Don Francis had learned that it was not enough to keep and eye on what was going on in your own family. You should know what was happening in the other family's business also.

Every Monday and Friday at precisely ten A. M. Joe telephoned the Don and spoke to him personally. The Don received personal and punctual calls like this from various cities around the country. He wanted to know what was going on, everywhere.

Young Joe decided that he needed a driver. A driver who knew all the streets and alleys around New York. A driver who could avoid the scrutiny of the police and still get from place to place fast. His driver would have to be loyal to him first. Such a man was Leo. Leo had been a New York cop for two years. He was of average intelligence. He could understand a plan when it was given to him, but he couldn't conceive or develop one. He couldn't be a planner, not a good one anyway.

When some senior officers were paid off to arrange to let a prisoner escape they arranged for Leo to take the fall for it. He wasn't sent to jail, but he was dismissed from his job. Leo never figured out just who was behind it or why. He only knew that his superiors and brother officers had screwed him over. Leo then drove a taxi for six years. He liked being outside on the street. When he needed a few extra bucks for something, he would work for a few weeks as a bouncer at some of the New York clubs. The clubs would hire extra help when they had a name act performing. This gave Leo information in and around the clubs.

When the clubs booked entertainment talent, they sometimes were expected to have a hairdresser and a cosmetologist available for the talent. Sometimes the talent had their own people, who toured with them. Sometimes the talent took care of their own hair and make-up. About half the time, the talent wanted the club to have someone on call.

Leo had been hired as an added bouncer for a club that had booked an act who wanted a hairdresser and make-up artist. The club's entertainment manager had lost his regular, on call hairdresser, to a broken arm from an auto accident. Leo just happened to be the guy standing there when the manager turned around. He snapped at Leo, "Get a hairdresser here. Now!

Annie grew up in New York, had just graduated from her cosmetology course and received her state license. She was out looking for a job. She had gone into a shop that was busy and tried to talk to the shop owner while the owner was giving a perm. The owner was saying that she was busy enough for another girl, but she didn't have another chair or sink to put her at. That's when Leo walked in. Leo had seen a shop in the neighborhood. When he came into the shop, he asked for the owner and explained that he needed a hairdresser right now and they would pay double the regular rate if they could just go right now.

The shop's owner wanted that double rate offer, but couldn't leave her old friend and regular customer, whom she was currently working on. All her people were in the middle of something. She looked at Annie and said, "Ok kid! Here is your chance. If you do good and I can get some repeat business out of this, I'll hire you. Do you have your scissors, combs, and such here?" Annie said, "Yes, I brought them." Gracie, the shop owner, said, "Good! Now go and do good! Come back when you're done."

Leo liked the looks of this young woman. Annie had fixed herself up for making a good impression for her job interview. Leo felt a little weak in his gut when he looked at her. He wanted to get to know her better, a lot better. At the club, she pleased the talent and that, in turn pleased the entertainment manager. He didn't care whom he had on call, just so long as they were there when called upon and that they pleased the talent.

The talent was booked for the week and Annie was there every night. Leo made it his duty to pick up and drop off Annie each night. Gracie hired Annie for this club work. Therefore, most of her work was done in the late afternoons and evenings for the club.

Leo and Annie started spending some of their social time together. Annie liked the way Leo treated her; like a lady. He was always polite and would help her with her coat, open doors for her and she liked the way she always felt protected when she was in his company.

Leo made it a point to ask around the clubs about their hairdressers. He was able to get a couple of good clubs calling for her service. Gracie was very happy with her new girl.

Joe had been hiring for the dinning club when he met Leo. Leo had applied for the position of security manager. Leo also told Joe that he knew the right girl for his hairdresser's position. Joe said, "Fine!" Annie was hired without even applying. She was now working regular and enjoying her position.

Over the next few weeks Joe learned that he could trust Leo to do what he had been instructed to do. Joe hired Leo to be his full time driver and security chief. Joe began to use Leo's knowledge of the other clubs to begin to chart the New York families' businesses. Where could a guy place a wager on a horse, or a ball game? If a guy needed a fix or a woman, where would he go? Whom would he see? Where is the gaming action in town? It didn't take Joe long to know where he could take the pulse of the New York families. Leo had become an important asset.

Leo wanted to impress Annie, so he bought a car. It wasn't brand new. It was a one-year-old Edsel. It looked brand new and it ran strong. What Leo liked about it was the fact that it was so different looking. It made him feel like he stood out from the crowd. He wanted to be able to take her to places. With the car he had the means. He spent a lot of his time wiping and polishing the car.

The club began to run like a machine. Everyone had a part and took care to do it right. Sammy was a club manager from Queens. Joe liked his look and his style of managing the club in Queens, so he hired him, at a substantial pay raise, to manage Joe's Place. Joe began to have time to do other things. He had department managers to look after all the details of running the various departments and reporting back to Sammy. Joe only had to check on them to keep them on their toes and to keep them honest. He and Leo began to go around town to the other clubs to see what was going on.

He learned where all the bookies were and for whom they worked, where all the vice cops hung out and which ones were susceptible to a little gift to look the other way, for a minute. In short, he was learning which of the New York families controlled what action and where. He also knew which ones were mean, which ones were tough, and which ones were the businessmen. Then he set about finding out which of the people in these families was feeling under appreciated. He figured that he might, someday, need to disrupt a family organization in order to get control of some of their action. One of the best ways, to do that, was from having someone right in the middle of, their own organization.

Once in awhile, Joe and Leo would take dates to the other clubs when they were checking out the other clubs operations. Leo usually took Annie. They were beginning to get close to each other. Annie was smart and it didn't take her long to notice that they were there acting like they were just enjoying and evening out, but in fact, the men were busy learning all they could about the operation of the club and it's people. At first, she thought it was just smart business for a club owner to know what the other clubs were doing. Then she began to notice that sometimes they would just sit in a car and watch who was going in and out of a particular place. Sometimes they would sit in a restaurant and drink coffee and watch what was happening at some other business or address nearby. She didn't know how that would figure into a club management profile, so she did what was natural for her; she asked about it.

Both Leo and Joe had grown so comfortable with her that Joe didn't hesitate to explain to her that he wanted to know about all the other business going on around them. He explained that it was important to keep on top of what was happening in the business community around the town. Not just the legitimate businesses, which anyone could see, but also the hidden businesses that most people didn't know about, even when it was going on right in their own pocket, so to speak.

As a club owner, you are on the cusp of the business world. If you didn't keep on top of the business, someone else would push in and push you out. This explanation satisfied Annie and she felt like she had just joined a secret club, spying on the underworld community. It gave her a titillation, which she found thrilling. That night, when she bathed, she noticed that the little fear, that she had in her system, caused her nerve endings to be more sensitive to her washing touch. She allowed herself to explore and enjoy the pleasurable side effect from that fear. She rather liked the extra sensitivity and she thought that fear might just become a regular thing in her life. If it felt this good coming down from it, then she was for it. She wondered if Leo might have the same reaction from the fear. She decided that her next encounter with fear would end with her and Leo instead of her and her fingers.

It was at this point in the story that I suddenly felt like I didn't want to hear anymore of what had happened. I stopped her and told her I needed a break. Earlier, I had wanted to get her a little relaxed with the wine, enough to take me into her confidence and tell me what she had held back for so long. I also wanted to get next to her skin and enjoy her wonderful sexual abandon. Suddenly, that urge had been displaced by a jealous anger at her for having had wonderful sex with someone else. In my mind, I knew that sex was something we all enjoyed and Annie was a beautiful sexual person too. I knew this intellectually, but hearing about it drove my emotions to react angrily.

"You asked!" Annie retorted, "And I wanted you to know about me too. If you cannot handle it, I'll stop. But, you have had sex before too. Don't blame me for being human. Don't be angry! Just, well, let's just get past this, and go on with our lives. I love you now, and I don't want to hurt you, but you should know what there is in my life that might affect you too. So, it is best, I think, for you to let me finish telling you what has happened and I'll leave out the stuff that upsets you. Ok?"

I swallowed a mouthful of wine and listened to her logic. I hated myself for being so small. I let go a big sigh, turned and looked into her beautiful, pleading eyes and told her, "Ok! Go ahead. And I'm sorry for acting like a jerk. I just don't want to think about you and some other guy having sex. And if you have to mention it, to tell the story, just lie and say it was terrible sex, so bad, that you never wanted to have sex again, until I came along and swept you off your feet. In that way, maybe my ego can handle it." I gave her a goofy grin and a shrug. She smiled a little smile back at me and said, "Sure! For some reason, I think I like it, that you can be a little jealous. Besides, the truth is, I have been so afraid, that I haven't let any man get close enough to me, to get emotionally close to him. You, somehow, managed to get past my defenses. I'm glad you did too. I'm feeling much more like a woman again, and yes! Sex with you is wonderful. The best ever." With that, she threw her arms around my head, pulled my face into her cleavage, and fell backwards, pulling us onto the bed, laughing.

I knew that she was probably exaggerating, for the sake of my ego, and having a little fun with me too, but suddenly I had this wonderful hardness in her hand. I was eager to continue with our mutual lustiness. I decided to let the story wait for the morrow. I think it is interesting to realize that my ego and vanity were so easily manipulated. It is wonderful, what a warm woman can teach a man, about a side of himself, that he never realized existed, before. Earlier, I had wondered if I was falling in love, by now, I was sure that I was.

In the morning, Annie suggested that we have breakfast brought up to the room. She said that she wanted to get this unspoken story over with. Then we would be able to get on with our lives without having this nagging fear between us. We needed to talk it out so that the ghost of her fear could be realized and perhaps then the thoughts that worried her would go away. I was bothered by her words, but I kept that to myself. I agreed and we called up room service.

CHAPTER VIII

TAKING CARE OF BUSINESS

The Don had Joe fly to St. Louis for a meeting. This kind of meeting didn't happen too often. It was reserved for those special discussions, which were never trusted to telephones, messengers, or anything, but face to face. When Joe returned, he was driven back by one of Don Francis' men.

Joe had brought back a pistol, a special pistol. An expert gunsmith put it together. It was a jewel of a machine. Its parts moved with the ease of silk moving on smooth glass. All its rough edges and corners were rounded and smoothed; its springs were light and responsive without being sloppy. It had a silencer, which the gunsmith called a muffler, built onto it such that it didn't appear to be an, add on at all, but rather an extra long barrel. Joe had gone out to a farm near St. Louis and shot up a few boxes of ammunition supplied by the same gunsmith. When he was very comfortable and accurate with it, Don Francis told him his assignment. He was also given an under the arm holster which had been custom fitted to the gun. The gunsmith made a few adjustments to the gun's grips, to fit Joe's hand better. Another box of ammunition shot at a set of targets, of varying distances, proved the precision of the gunsmith's work. Joe was ready to go back to New York and take care of business.

His business was with a man from Chicago, who had been partying in Las Vegas. He had said something to a casino owner, which was about to cost him his life. The Chicago man was well connected politically and he apparently thought that he could get away with insulting anyone he chose. The fact that he was connected only required that the hit be planned with a little more sophistication.

The manner in which a hit is done also sends a message to other interested parties. A professional hit is never a casual thing. It is laid out like a military maneuver. The first thing to determine is what kind of message is to be sent. If the target is simply in the way of your business plans and he won't be bought or compromised, then there is no need for anyone to know that he was killed. It should appear to be a natural or accidental death. An example might be an overdose of his prescription medication of even a simple overdose of a common, over the counter, analgesic. It is detectable, but not as a hit. It was just an accident. Some heart attacks, when there is no history of heart trouble, are caused by outside designers, but they are especially easy when there is, already, a history of heart problems. What if you want to let others know that the target has done something, which will not be tolerated.

Then you must hit him in such a way that everyone knows he has been killed for his error. If you kill him while he is in his private life, the message is that it was a private matter, but a message is still there for his associates to know that his actions were not acceptable. If he is killed in public, then it was a public matter, which is being settled. If he is disfigured about the head, in the hit, then it is because he dishonored a family member. He must be hit with extreme prejudice and then it should be done in a public place, so that all can see that he has paid for his dastardly act. The other half of the reason for the public act is, it is seen as a public declaration by the insulted party that the insult will not be tolerated. Any rogue, who is so rude as to insult the honor or pride of another man, will be duly dispatched to hell. A coward or a peon may have to take the abuse of such rouges, but this man, is not powerless to exact revenge and justice. This he does, for the world to see that he is indeed a man to be respected. Thus, his honor is retained.

After the message is decided upon, then the operation is planned around the message parameters. When and where can the target be approached? What defenses or hindrances are there? How can they be compromised or bypassed? Is a diversion needed? How can the plan work if various things go differently than the way it was planned? What modes of communication are needed to insure proper coordination under different circumstances? How do we shift from one plan to another and communicate that change? What and where are the escape routes? What type of hindrances can be positioned behind the escape to block pursuit? Should a patsy be used? A patsy is often necessary when there will be an intensive investigation after the hit. The public media will demand a perpetrator be brought to justice. Officials will not let up on an investigation until they can say to the public that they have fulfilled their mandate and caught the guilty party.

Joe's target was to be shot in the liver three times, to be sure that it was destroyed and to allow him to live long enough to know a lot of pain. To know why he was dying, Joe was to tell him, to his face, "This is from Vinny in Vegas. 'Roll a winner with these, ass hole!'" Joe didn't have a clue what this referred to, but apparently the target would and that is what the job called for.

The target was in New York to meet with some businessmen about some public works project. He was scheduled to be given a tour of the New York project and then return to Chicago where they might use some of New York's ideas in their own project. He would be staying at the Sheraton Inn.

Joe checked into the hotel as a businessman from Albany, in town to meet with some clients. After he was checked into the hotel, he moved around the building. He was looking into the stairways, timing the elevators, checking exit doors, checking into where and when the maids worked and stored their supplies. He even learned where the kitchen exits lead. What was in the basement and how can one hide in or exit from every possible floor? Where was the roof access and what were the possibilities of hiding or exiting from there? How responsive is the room service and do they stop serving at a particular time? When does the bar close? Where could you have a car stashed near the building for a quick exit without the hotel staff knowing about it? After his reconnaissance he went back to his apartment in Brooklyn.

He referred to the pistol as, 'the hardware'. He put it into his briefcase and returned to the hotel. The case was one of those, which had two handles. If you open the case latch and let go of one of the handles, and retain the second handle, the case is still secure in your grip and yet it opens allowing you to reach into and withdraw or insert something without fumbling. He had received information about when the target was expected to check into the hotel. Joe relaxed in the extended lobby, in an overstuffed chair. He looked like he was reading the newspaper while waiting for his client/target to arrive.

He had studied a couple of pictures of the target, which had been supplied by the Don also. He didn't want to actually read the newspaper. He had heard a story of a guy missing his target because his attention had become focused on an article, in the paper, and didn't notice his target, when he walked past. He had positioned himself to be able to see the check-in counter and the elevators. He was glad to see, that the elevators had a floor position indicator in the lobby.

If nobody got on the elevator with the target, then when the elevator stopped, that would probably be his floor. It was not always certain though, that someone, from an intermediate floor, had not stopped the elevator to get on it. You had to be careful. You could get on the elevator with the target, when he got on, and call for the top floor. This would give you better intelligence, but someone else could see your face with the target and remember it to the police. That is not a good idea. It is much better to be patient. Never be seen with the target or inquire about him. These things are usually remembered when you least want them to be. It is ironic, that these same people who remember seeing you and the target together at a particular time and place, can not remember their own mother's birthday. There they will be, in court, pointing a finger at the accused and swearing that they remember seeing, him and the victim together, just before the dirty deed was done. Joe was not going to let that happen to him.

Joe wore nondescript clothes and tried to hold the paper in front of his face without looking like he was holding the paper in front of his face. Most people, when they are hiding behind a paper hold it too high and too close. All you need is to have part of your face obscured. This way you can also see what is going on without the need to keep 'peeking' around the paper. Joe was so involved with doing everything right that he was almost startled when he saw the target in the lobby.

His blood pressure jumped and Joe felt himself, physically twitch, from the contraction of his muscles. Then he noticed that he had to control his breathing, to control the appearance of being relaxed. The paper's corner was beginning to tremble with the trembling of his hand. He couldn't stop it. He changed pages in the paper, to give his hands something to do, so that the trembling wouldn't be noticed. That worked for a moment, but then the trembling was there again. He decided to go over to the magazine rack and thumb through the magazines, just to give his hands something to do, other than tremble. The trouble with that was that the magazine rack was not in the right position for him to see the elevator floor indicator. When the target moved towards the elevators,

Joe took the magazine he had in his hands and walked back to his chair from where he could see the elevator floor indicator. All the while he appeared to be inspecting an article in the magazine. His hands were better, now that he was moving. The elevator opened and the target got on, alone. Joe relaxed a little. With his face turned at an angle, and the magazine held up before his face, he could see that the elevator stopped at the 8th floor.

He next went over and pressed the elevator call button. The elevator descended, opened and there was nobody on it. Joe felt good about the reliability of the information that the target was on the 8th floor. His breathing was normal now and his blood pressure was dropping to a more livable level. He took a deep breath and went to his room on the 4th floor.

In his room, he fell onto the bed and let out an audible, "Wow! Am I ready for this?" He immediately chastised himself for his hesitation. He got up and went to the bathroom to wash his face. He looked at himself in the mirror. He shook his head at himself and spoke out loud, "It will work and it will be ok. Just do the job, the right way, and everything will be fine." He thought the target would probably make a phone call to let his contacts in New York know that he was in town and arrange a meeting time in the morning. It was mid-afternoon and Joe thought the target would probably nap before showering and dressing for dinner. He didn't know when the target would go out for dinner.

He inspected the hardware and the briefcase. He took a pen and put it into his pocket. He practiced opening the case and withdrawing the hardware then returning the hardware to the case. It worked well. He left the case and the hardware in the room and walked the stairs to the 8th floor. There, he blocked the stair access door ajar, with the pen. The stairway was at the end of the hallway and he could see the room doors from there. He stepped back from the door so that if anyone looked at the door, they probably would not see him while at the same time, he could see out. Then, he did, what every soldier is well familiar with, he waited and watched, and waited some more.

There were a few people who came and went, but nobody paid any heed to the stairway door. He was prepared to look like he was casually walking the stairs if anyone took too much of an interest in the door. If anyone did see him, he would call off the hit for another future time. Nobody noticed.

It was about four hours later when the target finally appeared. He came out of a door, five doors down the hall on the left. He went to the elevators and went down without any companion. "Good!" Joe murmured to himself. After the elevator left, Joe went down the hall and looked at the room number. It was 810. He checked his watch. Then he walked back to his room taking the pen. He stretched out on the bed and tried to relax. He lay there for about 15 minutes. Then he did a few exercises and muscle stretches. After washing his face, he checked the hardware again. Then, with case in hand, he left the room. He repositioned the pen in the 8th floor stairway door and took up his position again. He noted that room 810 was on the other side of the elevator from the stairway. He planned, that after the target exited the elevator, assuming that he was alone, Joe would leave the stairway, behind him and move up to him, without him even knowing that Joe was there.

Two hours went by. Joe hoped that meant that he was having a drink at the bar before retiring. "Just don't bring up a bimbo with you." Joe thought. Every time someone came out of the elevator, Joe's blood pressure went up. He could feel himself perspiring even though the temperature was cool. His hands were damp and he kept wiping them on his trousers. Finally, the target stepped out of the elevator. When he turned his back to Joe and headed towards his room, Joe moved out of the stairway, as quietly as he could, with as smooth and relaxed a motion as possible.

He timed his approach to have him self beside the target when the target had his room door open. It worked, the door was open and the target was stepping into the room when Joe arrived at the door. Joe heaved his shoulder at the target's back. The target sprawled to the floor inside the room. Joe stepped into the room and quickly closed the door. Joe opened the case and took out the hardware. It felt, to Joe, as though it was taking twice as long to do as it had, when he had practiced it. The target was trying to roll over and trying to get oriented as to what was happening. He had drunk a bottle of wine with his dinner and his coordination was not good. The surprise had left his mind befuddled. It was a moment before he could realize that he was in trouble. To keep him from rolling over and seeing Joe's face clearly, Joe put his foot on the target's hips and pushed down hard. Joe snarled, "This is from Vinny in Las Vegas. Fuck a winner! Asshole!"

While Joe was pointing the pistol towards his liver, the target finally realized what Joe had said and the realization of his impending death scared him so badly that his bladder and bowels evacuated immediately. Joe pulled the trigger three times and backed away, until his back hit the door. The smell of the shit filled his nose and he was feeling nauseated. He put the hardware away and took out a handkerchief. He wiped the doorknob and opened the door. He looked out the door. The hall was still clear. He heard the man begin to scream behind him. He quickly stepped out and closed the door. He wiped the doorknob and walked as quickly as he could, while trying to look casual, toward the stairway.

He took the pen and opened the door as he looked over his shoulder down the hall. Nobody was there yet. "Good," he thought. The most dangerous moments were over. As he was going down the stairs he realized that he had misspoken the message. "Damn!" He mumbled, "Well, I'm not going to go back and say it again. I don't suppose it will make any difference anyhow."

When he got his room door closed behind him, he felt himself shaking and his stomach was still feeling nauseated. He washed his face and hands again, he combed his hair, straightened his tie and clothes. He made sure he had everything and left. He had prepaid for his room so that his checking out would not coincide with the incident. He simply left. The hotel staff wouldn't know just when he left. The key was in the room for the maid to turn in.

The target could only give a vague description of the man who had shot him. The police never had any idea, who the hit man was. The only thing they did figure out was that it was a professional hit. Done, for some vague reason over something that had happened in Las Vegas. The guy Vinny had an airtight alibi. Many upstanding people knew him, to have been in Vegas for over a month. The police knew what was going on, but there was nothing they could do. Nothing, but make some noise.

The man was in the hospital for a day, enduring a great deal of pain and the fearful knowledge that he was dying. He lapsed into a coma and died. Through the cloud of pain and painkillers, he kept mumbling, "Who the hell is Vinny?"

Joe was a bit of a nervous wreck for a few days, so he took a week off and went fishing in up state New York. He didn't want to be around the club or anyone. He found a fishing lodge where he could resort for a little while and get back to normal.

Vinny was very satisfied and Don Francis was very satisfied. When the Don was satisfied, then life was good for the boys in the organization.

CHAPTER IX

BILL COLLINS

B ill Collins was connected to the Irish mob through his father. He had avoided doing any business with them. He was, for the most part, a very respectable person. He seemed to really care about being a good leader, to the people who elected him to office. He had shown his character during World War II. He had done some rash things as a young officer, but when it was needed, he came through with courage and determination. He saved the lives of his men and himself. He knew his father's connections and business dealings had made the family wealthy. Now that he had the benefit of that wealth, he was determined to use it, to be the leader that his father wanted. He had determined to become the ultimate business and power broker. He was determined to be the President of America. He had this as his goal from before his first run for congress. He had known that everything he did would be done with the planning for achieving that goal. His father would not have wanted it to be any other way.

He chose a beautiful, educated, gracious, and socially well-placed girl to marry. Jennifer was the perfect choice. She and Bill hit it off right away. They really did like each other, even if it was a match made in a 'boiler room'. In time they fell in love and their marriage was a success. Jenny, as her friends called her, knew that Bill needed everything in their life to reflect what America wanted to see in their president. She accepted this as a part of the political life. She seemed to be happy with it and Bill. She knew that Bill would be spending a lot of time away from home on business trips.

Some of those first business meeting were for organizing the steering committee. This inner circle was composed of a few trusted and hand picked men who shared the same political, business, social, philosophical, religious, and cultural ideals. This circle included his brother and a few other men; they were associates of his father's. They would be called the Central Committee. They would be the brain that decided the strategies and tactics of the organization. They would guide the young man into the presidency and help steer his decisions once he was there.

Their father had introduced Bill and his brother to this small group of men. They were introduced as expert and experienced advisors. The young man was glad to have the help of such experienced men. He knew his limitations and he knew that he would be expected to make a lot of important decisions. He felt ill equipped to do this on his own. The committee of advisers gave Bill a lot of confidence that he could do a good job and come across looking very good.

Bill was to think that he was making the decisions and calling the shots. These men were only in an advisory role. As long as things went well enough for them, they were content to have Bill think so. Bill didn't realize, until years later, that he was just a figurehead, a front man for them.

At the next level in the organization were the people who shared the same political, social and business goals. This was the group that Bill would, in his turn, steer. He would use them like a nervous system. He would send out his desires for action through them and they in turn would get feed back from the outlying parts of the country and relay this to Bill. They were unaware of the existence of the Central Committee.

They thought they were the one's who, along with Bill, made the decisions about what was to happen, where, when, and how. They were the central body politic. They would form national, state, and county organizations. They started with the one state and a dozen local groups. They learned what worked and what was a waste of time and money. They honed and pruned their organizing skills and their skills at telling the people, what issues they wanted the people to consider and which position on that issue was the right one. By the time Bill was positioned to run for the presidency, they were already running like a clock.

They were ready for the big time event. The national organizations were formed and funded. They extended themselves into the other states and the counties. They organized several different types of groups. Some were political. Some were business or economic. Some were religious. Some were labor. Some were young social activists. Some were formed, for achieving one particular social goal, such as the environment or education or health benefits, or senior citizen concerns. All, from their individual perspectives, would come to the same conclusion; Bill was the man who cared about their issues. He was the candidate who would take care of their concerns. They were organized to rally around an issue or a political position and then declare themselves to be in support of Bill, for office. The people in each of the different groups thought that they were an autonomous group. They didn't know that they were a part of a large coordinated and controlled effort.

Some of the organizations were supposed to be openly organized from the national political headquarters. Others were to have the impression that they organized themselves, from the 'grassroots', as it were. They were issue minded and not political party oriented. It was the impression they and the press were supposed to have.

Some local leader would begin talking up some issue and then organizing the people who responded favorably to what he was saying. Other people would just start by talking to friends around a table at a bar, allowing himself to get louder so that the people around would hear. If they joined in on the conversation they were reeled in. It was a little like fishing. Some of the best bars were where the working people would congregate after work. From the construction worker's bars to the lawyer's watering holes and even the country club saloons, people will talk about what issues are on their minds.

It is amazing how many 'grass roots' movements were planned, blueprinted, and funded by the national headquarters. The only thing that was done at the local level was the organizing. The local person doing that was the designated person, who began and led the talk, and then allowed the locals to follow him. In the one-issue movements, the local leader didn't even mention the person they wanted to have elected. Their job was to take a stand on the issue and talk it up. Get the group focused on the issue. Really incite them, if you can. The issue itself had been selected and sent down to the leader by the national office. Then, when the mood of the country was right, the candidate would speak about the issue and take a stand, which just happened to be what the local group wanted to hear. They never did figure out that they had been, spoon-fed, their position on the issue.

Naturally, if a person had the other position on the issue from the candidate, then he or she never spent much time with the original group to begin with. The implanted leader would either turn them from their opinion or discourage their participation in the activities of the group.

Other locals, who were working for the national office, would keep alert to other 'grass root' groups, either genuine or implanted by the other political party. Their job was to join the group and report on, what the group was thinking and planning. Who were their leaders and, if necessary and possible, disrupt the movement.

What if there was a strong feeling building up in the community and the candidate was on the other side of the issue. Then sabotage was the order of the day. Peaceful demonstrations would become violent when somebody in the crowd, disobeyed the orders to remain peaceful. They became loud, obnoxious, rude, and started the violence, which was quickly responded to by the police, returning the violence. In a flash, the demonstration, in support of the issue of genuine concern, to peaceful voting citizens, became a riot and the leaders would be arrested. The media would portray them as a cult of over zealous, anarchists on a dangerous course of disruption of the public peace and our American way of life. It might be conceded that they had an issue, but we all had to agree, that this is not the way to address these grievances. The leaders, who had been successful in organizing a large group, now had arrest records. They lost standing in the eyes of the local community and as such, they could be successfully blocked from ever holding any significant office. They had been effectively nullified, as significant political leaders. Any other candidate who wished to employ them could be accused of working with known criminals.

There are different kinds of voters. There are the issue voters. They don't care about which party's candidate will do what for whom. They only care about what is his stand on their pet issue. They will vote for the candidate who espouses their side of the issue. They don't see anything else as being as important as the issue. They vote for the issue.

Then there are the party line voters. They see the party as a group of people with interests similar to theirs. By supporting the party they are supporting their personal interests. They may have differing opinions on various topics, but they think that, if they can work with the party for long enough then they will move up in the party hierarchy and gain more support for what they feel is important. For their support they get to meet the candidate personally, at a dinner, where they have to pay outlandish prices, to support the cause. They accept this as part of 'paying their dues' to be better socially and politically positioned to succeed in life. The parties hold that carrot very near to their noses so that they can smell it. They can even taste it, almost. The parties depend upon these stalwarts for their devotion. Keep them chasing that success and pulling the cart of the party. As long as they see themselves as being a part of something successful, they will keep pulling. They vote the party ticket, loyally.

Then there are the voters who don't have a special issue or a party affiliation. They vote, depending on how they feel about the candidate. It is almost a popularity contest with them. It is usually a mix of issues and feelings. They ask if the candidate will be a good leader, can he do the job? Does he look like a leader? Does he seem sincere? Does he have good values? Does he seem to care about us? Has he said something that I disagree with? How strongly do I feel about that anyway? Sometimes, people in this group, will just feel that they are disenfranchised by one of the parties and vote for the other one, even if they don't like that one either. Their thought often is, "They might not be for me, but at least they aren't against me. They may not support me, but they aren't attacking me, or my way of life. They will, at least allow me to continue being me and doing what I've always been doing without interference." The parties call these, the undecided voters. These voters are the most numerous ones, if they take the time or effort to vote. A lot of a candidate's efforts go into not saying something, which will turn these voters off. They vote their feelings.

Bill Collins had learned all these basic political tactics and strategies from his father and his father's associates. They had been in his environment, where he had been learning them, without being formally taught them, from early on in his life. His grooming for the office had begun early. Bill went to the right parties, attended the right schools, married the right girl, and now began the organization phase of the campaign. It would be a few years yet, before the public knew that he was an active candidate for the presidency.

Organizing, on this scale, required a lot of traveling. You had to meet the people who were going to do all this grass roots movement stuff for you. They had to be firmly in your corner, either by ideology or economics. It is always better to have ideology as the prime mover for these field people. They are easier to control and they are less apt to be bought off by the competition. They will give you their best, at all hours, for little or no money. They don't see themselves working for you, as much as they see themselves as your teammate, working for the same goal.

An organization of this size requires a lot of money. Most of your local people will have jobs for supporting themselves, so you only need to arrange for them, the support materials. A local office will be needed; it might be an old storefront. Also needed, are posters and placards, bumper stickers, and buttons, pamphlets for handing out, flyers for putting on cars, balloons and ribbons. There are a thousand and one different things that a campaign needs to attract the attention of the public. This will entail spending, and therefore raising, a lot of money. You do that by glad-handing a lot of people, a lot of people, who have money. The people, who have money, have it, because they don't spend it. They are capable of taking care of their self-interests with other people's money and are loath to part with money, except for furthering what they believe to be, is in their self-interest. To do this right, you will need to be introduced to them by someone they know and trust. What you avoid talking about is as important as what you do talk about. A thorough briefing, before you meet the person, is essential. You should be adept at leading a conversation around to a subject and also skillful at leading a conversation or a question away from an undesirable topic, without it seeming as though you have done so. A good man, or woman, at your elbow is often there to interrupt a conversation for some important phone call or meeting or on some other pretext, so that you can make a gracious exit from an otherwise inescapable and potentially embarrassing situation. Never allow yourself to be pinned down without an escape plan, because It is not wise to ignore, to give the wrong answer to, or to be rude to, the money people.

The money people try to get the money for you, from other people. These are the people, who are valuable to the party. They have become adept at getting other people to spend money. They know how to separate the green from the tight fisted. Although you spend your time with the money people, the money you get is from all the little people in town who want to further your cause or just want to get close to success themselves.

There are those people who have come into a lot of money rather suddenly. They are prime targets for the money people. They are much more ready to part with some of, or even a lot of, their money, due to psychological factors and poor thinking. It came to them easily and they believe more will be coming just as easily. They realize that it isn't bringing them happiness, so they try to do something that will give them pleasure and satisfaction by supporting a good cause and helping the human race.

They are on a quest to do something good and worthwhile. They have a tendency to believe this anyway. With the help of a good money person, whom they see as a peer and can therefore trust, they see the need, to use their money as a tool to do 'good'. The 'good', is sold to them in the form of the cause or the candidate. The expression, easy come-easy go, is well understood by the money people. The newly rich have not yet learned just how quickly large sums of money can just disappear.

People in the entertainment business are always targeted because of their vulnerability to political machinations. They make large amounts of money quickly and are naïve to the boiler room tactics launched against them to separate their money from them. They are invited to party with the influential political people and they run after the bait. They are like so many of the rest of the public. They like the idea of meeting and chatting with the famous and powerful people. It makes them feel as though they are one with the aristocracy and they have finally arrived to real success. Little do they realize that the whole evening is planned like an Amway meeting. They are told that 'their cause' is the cause of 'our man' and we really need to get him into office where he can do, the kind of good, that this country desperately needs done. The entertainment people are sincere about their cause. They make great spokespersons for the candidate, on the issue that is close to their heart. The fact that they are well known and loved by the public is great for the candidate. You cannot buy better political advertising.

CHAPTER X

LYNN MARIE

She was a beautiful, smart, and sexy woman and she wanted to be a Hollywood star. She had caught the eye of an influential man in Hollywood and he promoted her. She became the talk of the town and every guy in America wanted to have her. She had acquired her goal, but she didn't feel fulfilled. She had discovered that the Hollywood version of love was not the kind that satisfies the soul. She yearned desperately to be loved for being a person, not just a personality with a body. She wanted to have a sexy body, but she didn't want to be thought of as just a body. She was confronted with the realization that there is a difference between loving someone's image and loving the person behind the image.

She was invited to be interviewed on a local television talk show. She was to share her time on the air with the Great Jim Dion. The chemistry between them was immediate and strong. They were lonely people who were famous and successful while at the same time they were both desperate for personal love, as opposed to the public's love. When Lynn's part of the program was over and she left, Jim left also. They spent some time sharing dinner and then they spent the night together. They really believed that their love was the real thing. It was not long before they married. The press had a love affair with the lovers. They were America's favorite couple, Jim, the sports hero and Lynn, the sex goddess. America's two favorite people were now a pair. It wasn't only America who watched them, the world was aware of the pairing of this couple and wished them well.

Jim wanted his wife to be a wife on the model of his mother, a housewife. Lynn wanted to be the wife that Jim wanted, but she was also in love with the public's adoration to which she had become accustomed. When Hollywood called her, she went. She wanted to have the best of both worlds. Jim and Hollywood were jealous competitors for her time, neither wanted to share her with the other. Jim grudgingly accepted that the camera was a part of their lives. Then came the photo shoot that pushed the problem over the edge. It is probably the most famous picture of Lynn. Jim was present and almost lost it when the cameramen kept focusing their cameras on her panties and wanting retakes.

Every Sicilian in America thought of her as the wife of an important Sicilian and therefore a Sicilian by the extension of marriage. They were looking forward to the time when there would be children born to this couple. With such parents, they could not help but be beautiful and famous. They would be important people even while they were still children. The Sicilians had taken a large step in the enhancement of their position in America. She was their new sister. Every man and boy in America was wishing that he was Jim Dion. The boys were wishing they could be in his shoes. The men were wishing they could be in his bed. Some men are envied for their physical presence and talent. Some men are envied for their standing in their profession. Some men are envied for their fame and some men are envied for their woman. Jim had, what was perhaps the most unique position in the world, the envy, and even adoration, of men for all of these reasons. Jim may not have been the most powerful Sicilian in the world, but was certainly the most famous.

While Jim had Lynn in marriage, Hollywood controlled her publicity. It was through the media that she had the contact with her public and received the public's love and affection. She was the kind of person who needed and craved the approval of everyone. Jim was still getting the attention of the world and she wanted the public too. Hollywood won the war. Jim's love was wonderful, but it wasn't enough when she was starved for the attention of her millions of fans. The public's approval was like an addiction; she couldn't stay away from it for very long. In just a couple of years the marriage ended in divorce. They continued to be in love with each other for the rest of their lives.

Jim went on to win Best Athlete Ever and other awards. He was a sought after figure for his endorsements and the public always did love him. Through it all, his heart was empty. He would never take another wife. He was too much in love with Lynn. In his mind, she would always be his wife.

Lynn moved deeper into the Hollywood lifestyle in an effort to find the fulfillment she hungered for. She did more movies and the party circuit to keep her from being lonely. Because she wanted to be loved and appreciated so much, she became an easy target for Hollywood's influence peddlers. Some of these influential men were not from California. They had their clout in other parts of the country, but they would come to California for the business connections and the opportunity to party with the rich and famous. When they did come to California, they left their wives at home. Such was the case for the young politician from back east.

Bill Collins was in Hollywood to get some of that famous political support. Someone, who was trying to get close to Bill, in order to increase his influence with him, asked him if he would like to meet Lynn. She will be invited to a party. We will see that she is there to meet you. There was an attraction between the two when they first met. The sex goddess surprised Bill. She was a very intelligent woman. Not at all like the dumb blond she played in the movies. Lynn was surprised, that the political candidate with the privileged background seemed to be so sincere. He wanted to lead the nation to become better and accomplish more, for the people, than any president had done before. The attraction could be attributed to the fact that she was a beautiful, voluptuous, sex symbol who was also smart and from her perspective, he was a tall, open faced, handsome, and charismatic young man on his way to being the President of America. He was in town, without his wife. She was still searching for perfect and satisfying love. They left the party at different times and rendezvoused later. Neither was good or even satisfying at sex, but they enjoyed the closeness and at least the sex satisfied the primal lust. They enjoyed each other and the sex did bring them to a level of intimacy, which they enjoyed. They each had a sexual encounter trophy, which they could remember, fondly. They were both a little surprised to realize how much they had grown to like each other. They began to look forward to their time together. What was supposed to have been a casual sexual encounter for gaining influence had ended up being a match that ignited a romance and a downfall. They began to make promises to each other. He promised her, that as soon as he was ensconced in the Oval Office he would divorce Jenny and marry her. They kept in telephone contact. When their business travels got them near to each other they arranged a rendezvous. Politics makes for strange bedfellows; sometimes they can be fun too.

There are different management styles in business. Big crime is big business. Where there is big business, there is big money. Where there is big money, there is a political candidate trying to get some of it.

The heads of the different crime families each had their own way of doing business. Their individual styles were a reflection of many factors. A few of the wise old men realized that their organizations could not be limited except through the activities of the law enforcement men. If your business activities were illegal you would come under the scrutiny of someone in the law. Then your whole organization and your goals could be wiped out like a waitress wiping off a table covered in crumbs.

There are those who like the vice businesses. They like the thrill of being illegal, the image of the tough guy in the neighborhood. They liked the feeling of power they get when they can make somebody fear them and their wrath. To them, the thought of going legal is insane. Going legal wouldn't provide them with what they craved. Besides, they liked the vice business, because they were their own best customers. They wallowed in their own self- gratification. They partook freely from their own whorehouses and drug supplies. Their greatest thrills came from instilling deadly fear in those around themselves. For them, they had not gone into business to protect the neighborhood from outside vermin. They went into it for the thrills and the money and the power and the vice filled life, which they excreted from their very pores like sweat. In short, in comparison, they are the scum that makes a dump seem sanitary. They will never get huge in their business, because there are too many other guys out on the street who are trying to stop them. Forces from the law enforcement community and other guys who just want to move in on their action will be laying traps around them all the time. Sooner or later, they are going to step into one.

Some of the immigrants were prayed upon by the unscrupulous racketeers with the protection of one or two paid off cops. This incited some of the young men to form protective societies. They did not have much to start with and some of them turned to the vices to garner some capital. They used their money and their organization to help their people in the neighborhood. Then as the money and the organization grew, they either habituated to the vices or tried to take their business organization legit. Those men, who did have some decent quality in their souls, gave up the vice business as soon as they could get themselves extricated from it. It was an almost impossible task. The vice money was too easy and there where those characters in the organization who wanted that life-style, and they knew where the skeletons were buried, so to speak. If the half decent men let the vice business go completely, then the totally indecent men would take over that market and garner large sums of money and power to challenge the position of those half decent men. The best, most of these men could do was to separate their activities into two different worlds. Two separate organizations, with nothing to connect them except the man at the top. It is impressive, the diverse resources, at the disposal of these men. They could solve a business problem from where it was most vulnerable. They had learned a lot about managing an organization from the streets. These things are not taught in business school. Some of these men have become the heads of some of the wealthiest and most powerful organizations in the world today. Don Francis was one of these men. He preferred the legal business operations. They were the ones, which did not have a limit on how big you could grow. As long as you stayed within the limits of the law, nobody could wipe your table off.

Then, when you are big enough, you have the law modified to fit your business goals. Those laws, which restrict or cut into your profits, are targeted. The teams of lawyers and lobbyists that these men hire spend a lot of time trying to modify the law to have a null effect on their interests.

Bill Collins had sent a man to St. Louis to scout out the political money situation. He was to get the local money people organized and coordinated. Don Francis' name came up on the list of people invited to the fundraiser. The Don wanted to go to hear what this candidate had to say. When Bill met the Don, he was reminded of his own father. There was something in the way they commanded respect with just their presence. The calm, self assured way he moved and greeted people told Bill that this man was a force in the community. He wanted to get closer to this man for the benefit he might derive from his association. At this point, he had no idea that the Don had targeted him as well. The Don had been apprised of who this candidate was when he got the invitation to the fundraiser. He wanted an opportunity to get another politician beholding to him.

This young man had an impressive organization behind him. There was a very good chance that this man would be the President someday, if not in this election, then in another one. The Don was sure that this man would be elected sometime, and probably, in this election. It would be nice to have the President owing you a favor.

There was one little problem. Bill was a part of the Irish mob. A working relationship wasn't impossible, but it would be tricky. There had been cooperation before between the gangs. When the stakes were large enough and there was no threat to one another's turf, then cooperation could be had between two businessmen of like mind. After all, this was business, not a soccer match. The turf wars had been settled years ago. There would always be the pride of the gangs to contend with, but that, today, is just called competition. The Don watched and listened to the candidate. After this opportunity to evaluate him, Don Francis decided to support him. He was impressed with this man. He had what it takes to go to the White House.

Don Francis called Danny, the car man, and told him he was going to support Bill Collins in his bid for election. Danny was to be the coordinator for the Don's support, throughout the region, for getting the money and the votes. Danny's personal political inclinations were never asked about. It did not matter what or how Danny thought about it. It was business, just do it! It was done. This organization effort was taking place long before Bill's announcement to run had been proclaimed.

It took a couple of years to get everyone in place and the needed coordination working. The national headquarters had smoothed up the operation of the machine by using it to support a couple of other people for congress. In this functioning mode, some communication problems were discovered and corrected. The abilities of certain key individuals were reevaluated and they were moved around to put them into positions more suited to their skills. Some elements were added and others dropped. There would always be glitches when working with people. The machine was now operating well and the national headquarters had the control they needed. The cellular nature, of the functioning of the machine, helped protect it from the sabotage efforts of opposing parties. By the time the nominations for the presidency were announced, Bill and his machine were ready. It was a close fight. The other candidate was well known and popular. His election machine was running well also. The voting was close, but Bill won enough of the important states. To the public, it might have seemed like a year or less, of campaigning. The truth was, that it had taken several years of careful planning and working to get into the race, and then more years of effort and deal making to get to the White House.

When Bill woke up, the morning after the election, and learned for certain that he was the President Elect, it seemed to him to be a sudden thing. One day he was a candidate and the next day he was the President Elect of the United States of America. For a moment, he felt completely unready for such an awesome responsibility. It is one thing to go through the motions of getting ready, and another to be emotionally ready, to awaken to the truth of the situation. The emotional impact was soul shaking. For a few days, he was in a stupor. He went through all the right motions and smiled a lot, with his family, for the cameras. He made the speeches, which were incumbent upon him, but it still took some time for him to get his balance, within his own psyche.

Meeting Lynn a couple weeks later in a little cabin in the country helped release a lot of pent up energy. In his exuberance, he said a lot of things and she reminded him of his promise to divorce Jennifer and marry her. He said that he couldn't do that yet, because he had not as yet been inaugurated into office. He told her to wait a little while longer and when the time was auspicious then he would divorce Jenni. Lynn was very happy with the fairy tale fantasy of being the sex goddess first lady. She thought of herself as a Cinderella kind of person. She had come from being abused and now she would be the princess of the realm.

Political reality and the requirements of the Central Committee were far from their minds. Bill had not seen the subtle change happening. Later, he would discover, that the Central Committee did not work for him anymore. He was a puppet to them. They held all the connections, controlled all the money, and made all the important contracts. There was a token amount that he had direct control over. That was all for the public's eyes. Anything of any real importance was out of his control. He had to ask for their approval on many large deals. He was reminded of what it was like when he had been a boy, when he had to ask his father for money. Whatever the Central Committee decreed is what he had to do. They had allowed him to have many indiscretions in his lifetime. The revelation of these indiscretions could destroy him as a public figure and he knew it. He followed the instructions he was given.

We tend to think that we have elected a person to that great office. In reality, we have put an organized group of special interests into a very powerful position. The person is but the figurehead. The logo!

The possibility of divorce was so far out of the question that it shocked the Central Committee to hear him consider it. He was stunned by how forcefully they had stopped that idea. That is when he realized that they were making the decisions, not he. The last few months had seen his life take some dramatic turns. This last development had been totally unforeseen by him. Afterwards, he would ask himself, how he could have not seen it forming.

Lynn was given work, in Hollywood, to get her away from the East Coast. She knew what was going on and she began to keep a book on who did or said what to whom about what and when. She was still planning on being Mrs. Collins. She would just have to play the game the way they played it. With incriminating evidence, logged into a book. She was smart and patient. She prepared her moves.

Whenever he could, Bill would visit the West Coast and he and Lynn would rendezvous. She continued to expect big things from Bill and agreed to keep their affair quiet for his sake, for the moment.

The Central Committee was aware of all these meetings. They sent out the brother to talk to her to try to dissuade her. When they saw that she wouldn't be scared off or bought off, they decided that something more drastic had to be done to stop this affair. It was jeopardizing their invested plans.

CHAPTER XI

MARTA

She had grown up working in the sugar cane fields of Cuba. She had grown up strong and durable. She was also cursed to be pretty. There were always the boys who wanted to get her attention by acting silly. They were a constant distraction and she could not get her work done easily. Her real problems began when she was thirteen. That is the year that her father died. Now, there was nobody to be her guardian when she worked in the fields. There was a field foreman who would arrange for her to work in an area a little distant from the others. When he wanted to, and when he could find a convenient opportunity, he would grab her, drag her into the standing cane and rape her. He did this with impunity for two years during the harvest season. She was too small to put up enough resistance. Her family was a peasant family. They were accustomed to being abused by the privileged class and just tolerated it. Nothing was ever done to the privileged people anyway. Complaining would only bring more problems to the family.

When she was fourteen, one of the other young men in the field began to notice her. He was just a boy of nineteen. He tried to work his way nearer to her. He was close enough to see the foreman grab her and drag her into the cane. The situation was clear. In his rage, he ran into the cane behind them and while the foreman's hands were busy trying to control Marta, he cut him down with his machete. It was not over quick and easy. The foreman was knocked down and was bleeding badly from the deep cut on his back, but the wound was not fatal. The machete had hit too much bone. The foreman was struggling to stand and trying to figure out how badly he was hurt. Fear and rage formed him into a cursing, shouting, demon. He would kill them if he could.

The boy, Roberto was suddenly afraid. He started to move around to get between Marta and the foreman. He was ready to run away, when the foreman lunged at him, Roberto dodged. The foreman had lunged with such fury that he tripped and fell, grabbing at and ripping Marta's shirt off her. The boy saw her perfect young breasts and felt a fleeting excitement. He saw the fear in her face and then he felt compassion. He saw the foreman struggle to get up. Then, he was on his feet, his body still low like a bull getting ready to charge, his head down from the pain of the huge cut on his back. Fear, such as he had never known before, and rage seized Roberto. He instantly knew that his life and Marta's was forever ruined if the foreman lived.

He stepped around and swung the machete as hard as he had ever swung it in his life. His aim was accurate and the foreman's head fell to the ground. The body gushed a huge stream of blood and lurched forward toward Marta. She was instantly drenched in blood and the body bumped into her knocking her to the side as it continued on to kick and spasm and fall. The body continued to flail and spasm for a couple of minutes.

The boy was ready to run again, but he wanted to help Marta. He was appalled at the sight of her all covered in blood. Yet, still moved by her prettiness, her nakedness, her fear, and her vulnerability; he reached out and took her hand. "Come on!" He said, and turned to lead her back to where the other workers were. He stopped as he realized that as a worker he would not get a fair hearing. He would go to jail, be tortured and possibly even killed. He could not go back.

Marta would be vulnerable also for the foreman's death. He turned and headed through the standing cane toward the river and a life as a fugitive. Marta had observed the horrific occurrence from a state of shock. Her mind was not thinking. She was just watching the grisly scene happen around her without comprehension. She, at some level in her mind, knew that the boy had come to save her by killing the foreman and that now they were both in trouble. She followed the boy without ever asking herself why. She knew that she was covered in blood, but she had not realized that her shirt was now a rag hanging from her waist.

Nobody went looking for the foreman for several hours. By the time the body was found, it was almost dark. Roberto and Marta had gotten to the river and were six miles away. When they got to the river they both jumped in and washed the blood, the sweat, and the dirt from their skin, their hair, and their clothes.

Marta noticed that her breasts were bare. She examined the shirt and decided to keep it to repair later. Roberto was excited again at the sight of her breasts. She could see that even though he was being polite, he could not stop himself from looking at her. She knew the swelling in his trousers was indicating the level of his excitement. She turned her back as much out of her own embarrassment as well as being embarrassed for him. He then realized that she was embarrassed and took off his shirt and offered it to her. She was struck by this gesture. She was expecting to be raped again. Even in his state of sexual excitement and her vulnerability, he had not forced himself onto her. She began to respect this boy. The shirt was far too large for her. Roberto was a muscular young man from a lifetime of work in the fields. They were thirsty, so they found a spot on the river where the water was pooled and still. Here the sediment had settled and the water was clearer. They drank and then realized that they were hungry. Roberto knew a family who lived a few miles away. They went there to find some food.

The family had just put the children to bed when Roberto and Marta showed up. They were distressed to be confronted with this decision. They would be breaking the law to help fugitives, but they were people with whom they had worked and they knew how cruel the system could be. The woman was for calling the police and turning them in to get any consideration that they might be able to get. The man had known the boy's father and liked the girl's demeanor. He would not turn them in to the authorities. His wife would never go against the order of her husband.

She prepared some food for them and found a needle and some thread for Marta. Marta repaired her shirt while the woman cooked and the men talked about what they were going to do. They thought that the officials would go around to all the houses near the cane field, looking for them, during the night. Possibly even a house this far away. After they had eaten and packed some extra food in a cloth, they and the man went outside to be on their way. The man pointed and told Roberto where to find a spring of fresh water and a good place to spend the night.

It was dark by the time they headed out into the forest. Both of the young people had grown up in the countryside and were used to occasionally spending the night outside. This night they were feeling nervous. Roberto was able to make his way through the forest with the help of the moonlight. They found the spring about half a mile away. They drank a little water and found a spot, under a large fallen tree, where its root ball held the trunk up off the ground. Roberto still had his machete. They felt a little more comfortable with it handy. That was the best they could find for shelter that night, that and each other's arms. They fell asleep rather quickly. In the early morning they woke up and felt a little chilly so they snuggled a little more closely. That is when he became aware of her breasts pressed firmly against his chest. His breathing got a little heavier and she could feel his penis grow erect against her thigh. Her breathing got a little heavier too. She looked up into his face and kissed him lightly. He liked her kiss and kissed her back a little more firmly and caressed her breast with his touch. She had always been repulsed by the touch of the men who had touched her and their kisses had made her want to spit and wash her mouth. She liked the feeling she was having with this young man. His touch was thrilling her breast and made her want to enjoy it some more. His kiss was giving her a yearning in her genitals. She repositioned her legs such that her genitals were pressed against his leg and his erection was pressing high on her thigh. She kissed him firmly and rocked her hips against his leg. She was beginning to think that sex might not be such a terrible ordeal after all. His erection was pressing against her leg and it was beginning to hurt. She reached down to move it. He gasped and she thought she had hurt him. He said no, it was just unexpected and he never did finish speaking. They just let their hands and bodies do the rest of the communicating for them. They explored each other like the two kids that they were. She was the first for Roberto and he was the first to give her gentleness and an orgasm.

Later, in the morning, they ate the food they had in the cloth and drank their fill from the spring. Roberto explained to Marta as they walked down the hill in another direction, that they were to meet the man, from the previous night, on the road at a place where the road curved around the hill. The man had not said anything in front of his wife, because he did not know if he could trust her to not say anything if the police came by. When Roberto saw him driving up the road he felt like he was seeing a Saint coming up the road to save them. The man explained that he had gone by Roberto's house and explained to his parents what had happened and that he was well. He also mentioned that he thought Roberto and Marta made a nice couple. His parents had offered a quick prayer for the couple and another for the man for helping them. They sent along a jacket for Roberto and some under pants for the girl. That is all they had to spare. The man had told his wife that he was driving into town to see about buying a goat. The only difference was that she had assumed that he was driving into the local town; instead he was taking the couple with him while he drove to Havana to look for a goat. In Havana, they could disappear. The road was long, dusty, and rough. Roberto and Marta were very grateful to be so far from the field.

Marta found work as a hotel maid and Roberto found work in the hotel maintenance shop. They stuck with each other and their youthful lust and affection grew into love. Someone blamed the murder of the foreman on the new band of guerillas, which had come onto the island and were causing problems for the government. The police were so intently focused on the guerillas that were operating around them that they didn't have the resources or the inclination to look for runaway children. They never did conclude that the children could have done something so brutal. It must have been the work of the guerillas, trying to disrupt the sugar cane harvest.

A year went by and they were doing ok. They had many friends among the hotel staff. Roberto was now a bellboy. That was when the guerillas came into the city. In the confusion of the street fighting, Roberto went outside to see what was going on and he was killed by one of the guerillas who thought that his uniform was a policeman's uniform. Marta was three months pregnant at the time and the traumatic shock killed the fetus. She mourned for Roberto and their baby. She had never been a political person. She did not care who ran the government. She now felt her loss and blamed it on this bunch of guerillas. When it became clear that the guerillas were going to win the war for the island, she searched around and found a place aboard a boat to America.

There was an old neighborhood in Miami where the Cubans began congregating. It was beginning to be referred to as Little Havana. Marta found a place to live with some other refugees. The boys in the neighborhood were like a plague. They wouldn't leave her alone. She was still mourning for Roberto and her baby. She saw these boys as insipid, posturing, vain, and vacuous.

She was secure in America, but her heart died in Havana. She couldn't separate her love for Roberto and the baby from her memories of her island. She longed to go back to what she had in Havana. Life in Miami was dull, empty, and without meaning or hope. Life without her Roberto was just drudgery. She developed friends within the community. She had taken the opportunity to finish her secondary school work. She hoped that this would bring satisfaction to her life. It did not.

She heard some talk about a group of Cubans going to train in the swamp to take back the island from the band of renegade anarchists. The idea was like a seed planted in her. It grew to the point where she could no longer ignore it. Her only happiness, in her short life, had died in Cuba. She wanted to go back and get it. She was finding no joy or satisfaction in her new life in Miami. She felt that if she died in the struggle, she would be happier than if she stayed and lived, in Miami. It was a chance to avenge the needless death of her Roberto and her baby, who never had a chance to live.

CHAPTER XII

SOLVING PROBLEMS

The problems of office were always pressing and Bill was too busy to keep meeting on the West Coast. Also, the media cameras were swarming like flies. His visits became less frequent.

There was that renegade running amok on that island in the Caribbean. Bill did not care what he was doing there. He was not a threat to America. Bill received a request for a meeting from the honorable senator from Florida. The senator wanted the U.S. military to throw the renegade off the island. It had been a thoroughly corrupt dictator whom the renegade over threw and deposed. Bill was glad to see him gone. Where was the problem? The problem was, that in addition to tossing out the dictator, the renegade had tossed out the casino operations, the whorehouses, and many other very lucrative mob owned businesses were shut down and closed up. This renegade seemed to be intent on wiping someone's table off. He was a true idealist. That may be wonderful, socially, but it got in the way of business. He was costing the crime families, who ran the businesses, billions of dollars every year. The senator's point was that if this renegade is an enemy of business then he must be a communist. If he is a communist then he must not be allowed to exist this close to the U.S. We must send in the Army and throw that commie out. The American people will be behind us on this. This is a fight against communism. Bill thanked the senator for his report and said he would look into the situation.

Bill called in his cabinet of Secretaries and the CIA. He asked what was going on? What are their thoughts and ideas? They game played the various scenarios and decided to think about it and get together again tomorrow. Then he called the Central Committee and apprised them of what was going on and asked for their advice. He had been very respectful of their collective wisdom for years. It was only recently, with this Lynn affair, had he been at odds with them. He was still smarting from their action and insulted in his pride to learn of his true position to them. He had avoided calling them, because of spite, but he knew that now he needed their opinion. This was far too big for him to decide without consulting with them.

The CIA was expected to provide a good report on the activity in Cuba, but they did not have any reliable assets in the community anymore. There were mob guys who had to leave the island, who did know exactly what was going on and a lot of the associated details. The CIA met with a couple of these guys and struck up a relationship, so as to be able to get accurate and reliable information about an area where it was hard to get. The agency learned that if you were trying to get into an area illegally and carry on illegal activities, you had to think like a crook. You had to act like a crook. You had to make connections like a crook. The knowledge of all this would take time to develop. They didn't have much time, so instead of taking years to learn these things, they took the expeditious route and simply hired some of the crooks to show them how to do it. They were looking for a few good crooks. They needed someone to run some of the operations for them. From the crooks, the agency guys learned a lot of streetwise techniques about how to get a job done. The crooks liked working with the government guys.

The crooks wanted inside information in order to turn a government situation into a profitable venture for themselves. The crooks quickly used their access passes to steal a truck, loaded with high tech radio spy gear from the government. Then they let the agency guys discover that they had done it with the stuff that the government had provided. They were gambling that the government guys wanted their help enough to cover it up, which they did. It worked, because now they had what they really wanted. They did not care about the load of super secret radio gear, although that was really neat stuff. What they were after was something to compromise the government guys with. Now they had what they wanted, they had the keys to the cookie jar. The days of the mob and the agency had begun to work together as a team. What began as a quasi-military activity ended up being a comedy in the round. The mob guys would talk the agency into letting them train with some of the military guys, ostensibly, so that when it came time to take back the island, they could be in on the action on the ground. This ruse worked. What it did was provide access to liberate guns, ammunition, and explosives from the government's inventory and into the mob's warehouses.

Gunnery Sergeant Mike Beninni was ordered to duty in Florida. His orders were marked 'Clearance required, Secret'. Some agency guys met him, and a few others like him. Together, they had the duty of preparing, training, and outfitting some of the islanders for taking their island back. The islanders would need some good old military basic training and some of them would get an introductory course on extended reconnaissance missions. Some of those would get some spy techniques training which was to be supplied by the agency guys. Mike got along well with the agency guys. The agency men, shared with Mike, everything that they were going to teach the islanders. Mike was to teach basic training, and a sniping course. Setting up and executing an ambush was one of the skills to be practiced over and over again. For a couple of the students, there was a special combined techniques class. It amounted to planning, organizing, equipping, and executing an assassination mission. Several techniques were taught. Mike learned from the agency guys as much as they had to teach. He was already an accomplished sniper, but what was new to him was the advanced planning and coordination done at command and control level for an assassination. They also taught some techniques of surreptitious entry, which the military never employed. Mike was learning as much as he was teaching.

Some of the classes had women in them. For the most part, they were trained right beside the men. Some of them, because of their attitudes, were tough as men. In one of the loads of new recruits was a young woman who reminded Mike of a girl from another lifetime. After he had made them stand in line, he told them to sound off with their name. Her name was Marta. His mind recalled his girl friend from high school. Her name had been Martha too. Mike tried to ignore the coincidence and treated the trainee just the same as all the rest, but he caught himself watching her more than the rest.

They shared a beer one evening after the training day was done. They were comfortable with each other. The trainer-trainee relationship was different here. This was not the Corps. These were a bunch of civilians, foreign civilians. They were treated totally differently from the other groups Mike had trained. The training was tough and they did a lot of yelling, but the atmosphere was a lot more relaxed. This site was run by the agency and the agency wanted these people to feel like they were all equals, but for the dictates of the training. He and Marta gravitated to each other. Mike decided not to fight it, but rather to just enjoy the benefits of the camp. Marta was glad to have someone to hold at night. She was tough, but she also needed some emotional comfort.

Mike was honest and fair to her and, at night when they were alone, he was gentle and loving. She spent her nights with him for the duration of her training, except for when there was night training. His attitude toward her softened, but not the training. He did not know any other training style other than the hard, no quarter given, kind of training. She had to work as hard as everyone else and do all the trash details that everyone else did. Sharing her nights with Mike was the only thing different for her. Both of them knew it was only a short time affair. No promises given and none asked. They just enjoyed the moment shared between two emotionally scarred and yearning people.

She had a skill for, assassination with the knife, techniques. After another month of toughening, training, and targeting they were loaded aboard some surplus navy ships and set on their way to Pig Bay where they would begin the liberation of their island. There was to be a large supporting movement from the U.S. military, once they established a beachhead.

Lynn was feeling depressed. The studio doctor had prescribed some medicine to help her sleep. She did not like to feel depressed, but the studio said it would help her be more alert on the movie set if she could sleep better. Then there was the fact that Bill had been ignoring her. She had called several times to the White House switchboard and they were telling her that he was in a conference or a meeting or he wasn't in at the moment or he just wasn't available right now. What was he doing anyhow, trying to dump her? At times like this she would call her best friend and cry on Jim's shoulder. Jim was always there, for her, when she needed someone to talk to. He was caring and considerate and she took him for granted. He just kept talking about the two of them getting back together again. She was still in love with Jim while at the same time she was enamored of Bill. She still wanted to be the first lady, to be the Cinderella princess that she knew she was destined to be. When she felt abused by Bill she would allow herself to talk to Jim about getting married again.

He never gave up hope, because he never gave up loving her.

A week later, she flew to New York to help prepare a birthday party surprise for Bill. All the right political and business people were there. Everyone had been invited, except Bill's wife. At the right moment, Lynn came out and sang Happy Birthday to him. The cameras caught every embarrassed moment on Bill's face. He knew the secret love affair was out in front of the cameras for the world, and his wife, to see. Jenny was able to tolerate the thought that her husband was having an affair, as long as it was discreet and it didn't threaten her marriage. When it became publicly flaunted, then she was being publicly humiliated. She gave Bill hell. She threw a fit in the White House. There was screaming and some lamps were thrown. Lynn was hoping to push the situation along, to stimulate the divorce. If Bill and Lynn hadn't been living in the White House, it may have worked.

The Central Committee sent his brother to talk to Bill. Bill was given an ultimatum. He acknowledged that something had to be done. Something drastic! There was too much invested in his family man image, for it to be destroyed by someone, anyone. He gave the, go-ahead, and the brother reported back to the Central Committee. After a discreet amount of time had elapsed, Lynn was found dead. The news media was all over the story. The official report called it a suicide. That put an end to any police investigation, which may have followed. Any suggestion that the president was involved was squelched. The world famous, and greatly loved, sex goddess was dead. There were details around her death that didn't add up. There were discrepancies in the various official reports. There was no police investigation, but there was no end to the speculation. There are many, in positions to know, who say, "It was not a suicide." There was one person, besides the conspirators, who knew that Lynn did not die as it had been reported. He did not have the same evidentiary rule requirements that the courts have, for a conviction.

Jim Dion was grieved, as he had never known grief before. He took it as an extension of a personal attack. Someone had killed his woman. They had done this, openly defying the law and honorable behavior. They had dishonored him. He was angered more about the loss of Lynn than his honor, but don't think that he would have let the insult pass if it had been someone less. He was the Great Jim Dion and nobody was going to get away with doing this. Lynn belonged to the world and the world needed to have her murder avenged.

The murderers thought they were beyond the ability of anyone to touch them. They thought they could escape the justice system, because they had escaped the system for generations. They had forgotten to figure in the Sicilian Mafia and their long history of honor. Jim realized that nobody was going to do anything to avenge Lynn. If it were to be done, it would have to be Jim behind it. He swore on her grave that he would see it done.

Don Francis was relaxing with a few friends when he got the phone call. Jim was on the line and asking for a meeting, face to face. Don Francis told him to come out to St. Louis right away and don't bother checking into a hotel. There is plenty of room right here. He would have his driver pick him up at the airport. The Don was aware of the situation and was expecting to hear from Jim. He could even figure the reason for the visit, but he would let Jim do the talking. It was Jim's position of honor to take the initiative. Honor must be heeded among the Sicilian men.

The next day, Jim was in Don Francis' living room telling him what had happened. Jim told the Don, "Once a long time ago, you told me that if I ever needed a favor, I should just ask. I thought to myself then that there was no way in hell I would ever need to ask anybody for a favor, least of all, you. I know what it means to ask a favor of you, but now, now I need a favor. I need a really big favor. It is a matter of honor. I cannot do it without your help. I need to do it somehow. If I don't have your help, I'll find some other way, but somehow I will find a way. Please help me, for God's sake, for Lynn." The Don spoke deeply, slowly, like a father. "You are right to come to me Jim. I will help you. I have been expecting you. It will be my honor to help you. You know, of course, we accepted her as one of us when you took her to be your wife. She became one of ours. When she married you, she came into the Sicilian family. Now these sons of Irish whores are laughing at us. They have violated your honor and humiliated you by treating your woman like a common whore, and this, they have done before the eyes of the whole world. That was insult enough, but now they have gone and murdered her. This will not be forgiven!" The Don's voice had risen steadily in volume and strength until he was practically shouting with rage. "This will not be forgiven, no matter who they think they are. No matter what desk they sit behind. They will pay for this with their own blood. This is my solemn oath of honor to you my Sicilian brother. Their death for her death! They will die!"

The room vibrated with the strength of the shouted oath. Jim felt relieved. It was good to have an ally with the same conviction and dedication to his goal.

Jim stayed with the Don for a week going over some ideas and brainstorming about how such men could be approached. Jim had never been around this kind of venture before, so he didn't have much to offer except to say that he wanted the message to be clear. The world must know why. The Don patiently explained that there must always be some doubt. There must be, what the government people called, plausible deniability. People who understand honor will know that your honor has been restored. The other people, who don't understand honor, are not capable of understanding, even if you try to teach them. They don't even know that your honor has been challenged.

At another time, during their week, Jim had said something about when you do this. Don Francis interrupted and said, "Jim, you have to realize, I am not doing this. You are! It is you, who has the position of responsibility. You are taking the responsibility for setting the scale of justice back on its balance." Jim was surprised and unprepared for what he thought he was hearing the Don say. He argued back that he was not familiar with, how to kill any thing. He had, once upon a time, along time ago gone through army basic training and he had shot targets, but he had no experience in really killing anything. He argued, not because he was not wanting to or that he was unwilling to go to jail, but he did not know the first thing about shooting a person. He had spent his life playing baseball. Even when he was in the army, he played with baseballs not guns. The Don said, "That's ok! You only have to be the one to initiate the action. After all, these guys not only challenged your honor, they have challenged all of us. By killing one of us, the whole Sicilian community has a debt of honor to reclaim. We can do this as a family thing. Un cosa nostra familia."

The Don continued, "I will take care of the details. Jim, I don't want to discuss this with you farther, because only the people doing them should know the details. There is less chance for someone to accidentally tip someone else off about what is going on. I do want to thank you for coming to see me asking this favor of me. It is a good thing. I once told you to just ask if you ever needed a favor. I never thought you would ask me to kill the President. Now you have, and I can not say no." Then the Don chuckled and said, "There really is nothing small time about you is there? Not even a favor." He laughed again and shook his head as he strolled away into the kitchen.

Don Francis made a few phone calls and a week later, a group of men were meeting. "We must set up several other possible suspects, each more probable than ourselves. If necessary, we will even give them a pigeon." Uncle Benny had the attention of the room, "No! Thinking about it again. We will have to have a patsy, there is no way to clean our trail without a patsy." At this meeting there were a couple of guys from Chicago, a man from Detroit, another from Las Vegas, New York had two men, and finally there was a guy from Miami. They were the recognized best in the business in America. They were having a planning session. Don Francis had called the meeting to order. They were to map out some basic ideas about who and how to do it. Families, which usually, only reluctantly cooperated for the sake of business, now found themselves with a common goal.

The Irish had gone too far. Some guys in the families didn't like having an Irish mob guy in the presidency, with his brother in the office of Attorney General, because they feared that now he would come down on them and take over the best turf for the Irish mob. It was one thing to compete for turf, but to bring in the federal lawmen as your own personal army was cheating. He was definitely in the position to take over and make it look like it was a law enforcement campaign to clean up the country. All the while, shifting the balance of power and money to the Irish families.

The man from Florida said, "We will have to pay a lot to our friends in Washington to make sure that the follow up investigation goes away from us." Las Vegas added, "As long as we see to it that the job is done with a lot of confusion, they will be free to form the needed conclusions, to support the position we want them to."

One of the New York men said, "This is way too important and high profile to let anyone but our best people handle it. We will keep the whole team to just a few people. We will use cellular organization, so that any one person will know only one or two other people. They will not know what is going on in the other parts of the plan or who is there to take care of it. They will know only their one small part. Only after the job is done will they be able to figure out what they were a part of and then they won't have any evidence or names to give to the police if they should ever be turned against us. The only contacts they will have will be with the person who gives them their instructions and pays them off. If anybody gets too nosey and learns more than they are supposed to know, then they get whacked.

The other New York man said, "Don Francis, we all want to share in this, but we need to put this on a very secure basis. What I mean is, this is too big for a slip up on the part of any one of us. Therefore, let us each give some advice in the general way that we think this might go down successfully and some precautions to watch out for. Then, we should choose just one of us to run it and keep the rest of us on call as needed. We won't know any of the details, but all of us can claim some credit in it by virtue of being here to help plan the overall attack. That will satisfy our people." Then he sat down.

The Florida guy wanted to know how they were going to decide who was going to run the operation. The Detroit man spoke up, "It's clear, some of us have been doing this longer than the rest and will be better able to hold their mud. I don't think it should be a straw vote. We won't get the best guy for the job that way. I think Benny should do it, besides he is the oldest one here. The New York man wanted to know what that had to do with it. The Detroit man replied, "With this hit, there is going to be the biggest investigation you ever saw. The pressure on the cops, to find the guy who did it, will be enough to blow this country, wide open. The Feds too, will be giving it everything they have to nail somebody. Whoever does this might have to do him self if the heat gets too close. Or we might have to do him ourselves for the sake of all of us. Besides that, Ben is perhaps the best qualified to do it."

The room was quiet for a moment as they all realized the truth of this. Benny spoke up, "That is right.

That is why I should have the honor of doing it. I am the oldest guy here. I have been doing this for more years than some of you kids have been alive. Therefore, I owe more to the organization and the organization owes more to me, than you youngsters. Also, I don't have any wife or kids, so if it becomes necessary, I can take the out."

The room was quiet again for a little while. Florida spoke up, "What assistance can I give you Benny?" There wasn't any vote. Everyone just accepted it. Benny would be the hub. Everything would radiate out from him. Most of them were relieved to be off the spot. Benny was thoughtful as he spoke. "I will need a couple of things, but let's have some lunch while I think about it. We will talk again in two hours." The men went to lunch at Johnny's Steak House. To observe them, would be to observe any group of businessmen at lunch. They talked about their kids and their wives, their cars and their sports teams. Nobody, observing them, would have any idea about the topic of their business. They were just a group of businessmen having lunch on a rare, nice day, in Chicago.

CHAPTER XIII

MARTA RETURNS

It was another three weeks before Marta was bussed out to the training site with twenty other Cubans. She had been required to visit a doctor and get a qualifying physical examination. After that she was given an interview. A man from the American government examined her papers and asked her about why she wanted to go to fight a war and possibly get killed. She passed all her tests and was allowed on a bus that took her and other Cubans to the training site in the Everglades.

There was an American Sergeant in command of her training platoon. She felt herself admiring and respecting him. He was not a superficial poser like the men in Miami. He had a quality about him that reminded her of Roberto. He was older, but that did not alter the attraction. After watching him for a few days, she decided that it was his lack of selfish intent that was like Roberto.

As she trained, she was aware of him watching her also. That was his job, to watch and train, but there was something in his face, which told her that he was interested in her as a woman also. He never said anything to her, except in the line of duty and training. He was not a man to take advantage of his position of authority. One day, during a break in the training, she approached him. She smiled and asked if he knew where a girl could get a beer after the training day was over.

That evening, she met him at the cook's mess tent and they shared a beer and talked. He mentioned that he had noticed a similarity between an old girl friend and herself. She mentioned that he reminded her of an old boy friend and then they both laughed. With the laughter, they were both suddenly comfortable with each other. They allowed themselves to become intimate, knowing that it was just for the moment. During the training, she thought the time was passing slowly.

A few weeks later when she was boarding the troop landing ship, she looked back upon the last weeks as having passed like a mirage. She tried to get into a corner of the landing ship, where she could brace herself against a bulkhead. The ocean swells were making the little ship bob around and most of the people were getting seasick. The deck was slippery with water and vomit. The smell was that of a bunch of people packed in tight and scared of what was about to happen to them. The vomiting wasn't just from the heaving of the sea. They were afraid of going into battle and the uncertainty of their future. In the next hour, their lives would be totally different from anything they had ever experienced.

Everybody was so much bigger than she. Before, in training, the men had given her a little consideration because she was a woman and smaller than they. Now, everyone was so immersed in their own concerns and their own thoughts that they took on a palpable quiet. She began reminiscing, as she was adjusting her gear, to be a little less uncomfortable. She was jostled by the movement of the ship and the men around her as they all were trying to get decent footing and comfortable in the packed 'can of bodies'.

She recalled the days in the fields with Roberto and their first time together. She recalled the little room they shared, at the hotel. She thought that in the depths of poverty she had been happy. Not because of the poverty, rather in spite of it, because there she had also known love and mutual commitment. She smiled at the thought that she, with her nothing, had found what so many rich people were still seeking to find with all their money and all their vain scrambling. She had found contentment in her life, even if it had been for only a fleeting moment in time. She was satisfied to have shared love and goals with a good man. Now, she had another worthwhile goal to strive for. She was here, with others, to take back their home. She knew when the efforts of her actions were consistent with the goal of her heart, satisfaction was realized. She felt very scared, but happy and satisfied with herself as a woman, as a person, and as a human being whose life matters.

The little ship's commander blew a whistle. Everybody began tightening the straps of their equipment.

The air was foul with the stench of vomit and fear. The rocking of the ship and the fear in her gut caused her stomach to spasm. She had not eaten anything before the trip, but her stomach wanted to churn anyway. She looked around at the faces of the men and the few women near her. She could see their eyes rounded with the fear of the coming moments. Nobody was talking. She imagined that they were all involved with their own memories of loved ones left behind. She knew some of them from their training together. The ship's engines went into full throttle.

The ship was charging the beach. She braced herself for when the ship would come to a sudden stop. She knew that she would not be the fastest in the run to the beach. She didn't want to get run down. She planned to run to the side as soon as she was in the water, so the surging platoon could move quickly to the beach without her being in the way. She would run to the beach as fast as she could. There, she was to help the radioman run his antenna wires and provide protection to him while he put up his equipment. She remembered her nights with Mike and his training. She smiled as she thought that she was luckier than most. She had known two very good men in her life. She was doing this for Roberto, their baby, and herself, but she was doing it, as she had been trained to do it, by Mike. Her convictions were from Roberto and her methods were Mike's. Something of both of these men, were with her on this dawn.

She checked her rifle again. She looked around again at the faces around her. She saw the fear; she also saw the determination. Mike and the other Americans said that they would be here, as soon as they had established the beachhead and gotten the radio message back to them. She knew that some, in her platoon, would die today. She put her mind on Roberto and her island. She spoke out loud to her island and to her memories of Roberto, "I'm coming Roberto. Cuba Libre!" The ship grounded to a sudden stop on the bottom of the surf. The landing ramp fell and they ran for the beach. Some were stumbling in the surf. She was finding it difficult to run as hard as she could through the surf while wearing combat gear and carrying all the extra things she would need. There was food and water and ammunition and grenades and a shovel for digging a hole and her rifle. It was all heavy and the surf was pushing her around. The sounds of the battle began and she was surprised at how the pressure waves from the exploding shells pushed against her body. She could hear the fast whistle as bullets and shrapnel pierced the air near her.

She was expending all her effort to push through the surf. Suddenly she felt a dull abrupt pull on her leg. She continued to move forward to take another step. She felt herself falling forward into the surf. The leg was gone. It had been blown off by an underwater, anti-personnel mine. She fell under the water. She tried to get up, but the equipment held her under. She struggled to hold her breath while escaping from all the equipment. The exertion of trying to run through the surf with all that gear had left her short of oxygen. She had been gasping for breath before she fell under the water. She could not hold her breath any longer. She felt her air leave her lungs. She tried to scream. She did not want to die so soon. "Not yet," she tried to scream, "Not yet' as she died. Her blood mingled with the seawater and in the midst of the horror and the chaos of battle, her blood gently washed up and caressed the island she loved.

ENTER THE HEART

CHAPTER XIV

MIKE HAS ENOUGH

When Mike and the other training cadre heard that the landing had been a disaster they wanted to know what had happened to the support the US had promised to give to these people. They learned that the President had, at the last minute, changed his mind and not sent in the support. Mike felt as though he had taken a punch in the solar plexus. He was not able to comprehend how we could send in dedicated people to their death and then go blithely along our way. He felt a comradeship with all the people he trained, but his mind was full of Marta. She had been one of the most wonderful and dedicated women he had ever known. He had not understood how much she had come to mean to him in the few weeks that they had been together, until he realized that she was dead. He went down to the beach and spent time walking and thinking about her and some of the moments they had shared. He walked into the water and touched the water and got a strange feeling like he could almost hear or feel her blood crying out to him from the sea, "Why? Why did you abandon me? Why did you promise? Why?" When he experienced that feeling, he broke and cried. He had not cried since he had been a boy.

He hated what he had done to her. He felt like he was responsible. He was the personal representative of the United States of America to train those brave people. He felt that the President had let him, the Corps, and whatever America had stood for, down. He hated himself for what he had been a part of. He felt dirty. He focused his anger on Bill Collins. That son of a bitch could have saved them if he had just called it off a little sooner. He was haunted and infuriated that he had been used to help slaughter those people.

That was when Mike decided that he had to retire. He had one year and five months to go on his current obligation. He had enough years in to retire. He had been proud to be a Marine. He had been proud to be an American. Now he felt sick to his stomach when he thought about what he had been a part of. It was time to leave. He was assigned to duty as a drill instructor for the balance of his term. He still cared about building good marines.

CHAPTER XV

MIKE IS RECRUITED

Just before his term of enlistment was up, Mike read about Lynn's suicide. Lynn and Marta didn't look anything alike, but Mike was reminded of Marta's death when he read about Lynn's. He thought that perhaps it had something to do with a sudden and seemingly useless death of a beautiful woman.

After his retirement, Mike visited his childhood town. He went by the house where Aunt Mary used to live and he recalled her motherly love for him. He remembered her homemade sugar cookies and smiled at the pleasant memory. She had died of heart failure some years ago. As he drove around, he found himself driving by Martha's old house. He wondered what had ever happened to her. He had never forgotten her. He hoped, with all his heart, that she had found happiness and a good life. He thought he was feeling too maudlin so he drove on. He thought that his driving around and looking at all the old childhood landmarks was kind of like browsing through an album of his past. He wondered if Uncle Benny was still alive. He remembered hearing something years ago that Benny had moved to town to be nearer to Mary when she became invalid. He had taken her wherever she wanted or needed to go. She went regularly to church, to pray for the souls of the people in her life. She had prayed for Mike and she had prayed for Benny and Mike didn't know all for whom she prayed, but he was sure the list was long. After she died, Benny had kept his home there. He liked the little town. It had good air and good people. Mike stopped for coffee at a café. While he was there he looked in the phone directory and found Uncle Benny listed. He called and stopped by to pay his respects.

Uncle Benny was pleased to see Mike and he invited him to stay with him for a while. Mike commented on Benny's apparent good health and vitality. Benny laughed and said it was the result of living a good life. Mike did not have anything else to do right away so he moved into Uncle Benny's spare bedroom. Over the next few days Uncle Benny and Mike told 'war stories' and laughed at each other's amusing anecdotes. In the evenings Mike would drink beer and Uncle Benny would drink red wine. Then they relaxed enough to share the stories that weren't humorous. It was during these times that they learned more about each other. They learned about what they felt was important. They learned what it was that reached into their hearts and made them want to cry. What moved them to want to act? What incited them so much that they were ready to face God and plead their cause? They talked about war. They talked about politics. They talked about the families. They talked about Cuba and the fiasco at Pig Bay. This happened over several nights and several bottles of good 'tongue oil'.

After Uncle Benny had assessed Mike's character, he told him how he was glad that he had become the man that he felt he knew many years ago. Uncle Benny then talked about how the families felt about Bill Collins murdering Lynn and the challenge to Jim Dion's honor. Mike perceived the shift in the conversation. They both had been drinking and relaxing, but both men knew how to drink and keep their minds clear. Mike wondered what Uncle Benny was steering towards. He took a pull on his beer and just let Uncle Benny lead the conversation. Uncle Benny went on to say that Jim had decided that he was not going to let the son of an Irish bootlegger get away with the murder of his wife, even if he was the President. In fact, it was precisely because he was the President that it was necessary for Jim to take the action.

If Bill weren't the President, the justice system would take care of the matter. Being President is good. Having your brother as the Attorney General is very good. He was now, untouchable, by the system. Being popular with the people is insurance. Because Bill was the President, nobody was ever going to do justice for Lynn. If Lynn was ever to have justice, it would have to come from some place other than the law enforcement community. Jim had been her husband. The position from whence this justice had to come was from Jim. Jim was not going to fail, the woman he loved with his whole being. Jim knew there was only one way to get the justice the situation called for. Jim was not impotent to handle his responsibility. He had resources and he was using them.

Uncle Benny paused to see how Mike was receiving this. Mike was recognizing the truth of what Uncle Benny had just laid out for him to view. "Uncle Benny," Mike began, "You wouldn't be telling me this if you did not know that Jim felt this way. For you to know that he wants justice means that Jim has come to the family for help. He has never mixed in with the business of the family and therefore does not have the means of doing this thing on his own. The family has granted him this favor." Mike was trying to figure out the scenario as he was talking. It was like doing a crossword puzzle. One answer filled in the blanks for another answer. Just keep walking the dog, sometimes you pulled the dog, and then the dog pulled you. Mike kept pulling and was pulled along by the dog. The crossword puzzle was filling in. Mike continued, "Since the fox is still alive, the job is not done yet. Therefore, the mission is in the planning stage. Since you know that Jim is doing this thing, with the family's help, then you are in on the planning. And you are telling me about this situation." Mike stopped as the answer on the next line came into his mind's view. "You old fucker! You want to ask me to be a part of this. Don't you?" Mike was decidedly more animated as he moved around the room. He thought that the idea was incredulous. It is one thing to think about something like this, but to actually contemplate doing it was stupefying.

Uncle Benny went into the kitchen and returned with another beer for Mike. "Why not give it a couple of days?" Uncle Benny spoke very nonchalantly. "Relax! Hang around town for a while; think about it and what it would mean if we don't do this thing. Then, when you have decided, let me know. Don't take too long. I do have to keep this thing going." Mike spoke up, "Look, Uncle Benny, what you are asking is-is, well, I." Words had never failed Mike before, but now he was being asked to consider something, which he would have never considered on his own. "Uncle Benny! Look! For the last two plus decades, I have been in the military service to my, to our country. He is, or was, my Commander in Chief. I have sworn an oath of allegiance to our country and our constitution. To even contemplate this act is treasonous. You know, or you should know, that I love my country and I love what it stands for. To ask me to be a part of this is to ask me to cut open my veins. It is to ask me to just trash everything that I have stood for and fought for, over my whole life."

Uncle Benny placed a gentle hand upon Mike's shoulder and said, "It's because you love this country and what it represents that you should think about what kind of man it is in that office. He is like that white sepulcher, which Jesus spoke about. He is perfect and clean for the world to see, but we, you and I and a few others, know that on the inside he is full of death and the stink of death is on him." While Uncle Benny was saying that, Mike was remembering Marta and all the others who were beside her on that beach in Cuba. Uncle Benny continued, "He led many people to their certain death when he abandoned them in Cuba.

Now he has murdered a woman just because she believed, his lies to her. He isn't the nation or what this nation stands for. He isn't the constitution upon which this nation was formed. He is just a charismatic, weak, character who murders people who might embarrass him.

He is hiding in that oval office. Is that what you took an oath to protect?"

Mike was still thinking of Marta. He wondered how she was killed. Did she make it to the shore of her island? Did she have time to know that she had been abandoned to die? Did she blame Mike? Mike turned to Uncle Benny and told him that he understood how he felt. "I'll need a little time to sort out my thoughts and feelings."

The next morning Mike drove around to get his mind clear. Sometimes, when he had something weighing heavy on his mind, he found that just going for a drive helped him relax and turn the problem over in his mind. He drove up to Cedar Point and got out and mingled with the crowds. He listened to the people as they went about having fun. The screams of the kids, as they hurled around on the roller coaster and the other rides, kind of made him wish he had taken the opportunity to raise a family of his own. He thought it was probably just as well that he hadn't. What would he do, now that he was out of the military? What kind of work would he like to do? He had liked what he had been doing. He only got out because of the shame he felt for the debacle he had been a part of. He had always liked the military and the service to the country, even when that life had been in the mud or in the cold. Even during those times when there had been an enemy shooting at him. As miserable and as stressful as it had been at times, he still felt it was satisfying a deep urge, from within him, to do the right thing and protect those who could not protect themselves. He almost laughed out loud for a moment when he realized that, yes! He enjoyed the feeling of being somebody's hero. He did not need or want a medal on his chest or a parade. He only needed and enjoyed the feeling of satisfaction he got from doing a miserable job, which needed to be done, for the peace and well being of the people. When they thanked him, that was reward, but he did it for his own need to be an honorable man. Mike had always had these feelings; he just never had taken them out and examined them before. With these thoughts, newly revealed and recognized, Mike knew what he had to tell Uncle Benny.

As he was driving back, he was thinking about his oath. 'To protect and defend against all enemies, foreign and domestic.' He thought it was interesting how we always think of the enemies as being foreigners, but how we are pledged to protect against domestic enemies too. Sometimes the enemies are smart enough to occupy those offices. They know that from there, they can do the most damage to what we value in this country. Truth, and Justice for all!

In our striving to protect those offices, sometimes we are protecting our own worst enemies. We give our enemies the shielding, to act with impunity. Mike thought that the men who drew up the Constitution and the Bill of Rights were wise enough to have allowed for just such a situation. However, when, with the authority of their office, they can marshal the law enforcement and the military forces against the people, then the people will have to be able to defend themselves and their valued way of life, by the force of arms, if necessary. "Thank God for those wise men." thought Mike, "I do believe this is the only way to rid ourselves of this fox, in our hen house.

Uncle Benny was relieved and glad that Mike had decided to help. If Mike had decided not to be a part of the plan, then Uncle Benny would have had to kill him. He knew too much to be allowed to live without being a part of it.

Uncle Benny liked Mike and would not have liked doing it, but a man has got to do, what a man has got to do. Uncle Benny thought he chosen the right man, but there is always a chance that he will say no. In about any other plan, saying no is ok and there are no repercussions. This plan was too big and too important for that. If any one knew about it and they were not a part of it, they had to die. Period! End of sentence! Nobody wanted to compromise this operation.

That afternoon, Mike and Uncle Benny began to game plan the hit. Uncle Benny knew that Mike was a sniper and thought that this should be the way the hit was delivered. To get too close is to get caught. There is no need for that. Somebody does need to get caught, yes, but not the real hit man. That is what patsies are for. They are disposable. Explosives were ruled out for various reasons, but the main reason was because they wanted to deliver the message. The message had to be clear. The world should know that, this which is done in this manner is a matter of honor. The message is: "You have taken a life, 'in my face'. Now, your life is taken 'in your face.' Honor will be accorded.

Mike asked about whom they might set up as the patsy. Uncle Benny had a few people he would have liked to have set up, but none of them was believable as the patsy. Mike thought that they should set up more than one patsy. Maybe, layer them, like an onion. The

Enter The Heart

best detectives in the country would be trying to unravel this. Give them a series of dead ends and cutouts. If we can have some redundancy in patsies we will be better protected from the unforeseen occurrence. What if our patsy doesn't hear his alarm clock and is late? What if he gets a traffic ticket and is late? What if his car breads down or his girl friend picks that day to have it out with him or any one of a million things happens? I think that for the level of importance of this hit, we should have at least three patsies and each of them should have a patsy to take the heat behind them. There should be a cut out at that level. When one of the patsies is picked up, the others get to go home scot-free and the police never even know about their existence. Each of the patsies will have a different position and background.

While Mike was focused on throwing someone off his trail, like a sniper would, Uncle Benny was focused on finding someone else to take the heat, like a gangster would. He was asking, "Who has a beef with the President? Who would like to see his demise? Who would have the ability to do this? We need to give our patsies some slant that will lead the investigation to those people and away from Jim. For that reason alone, we need to wait until Lynn's death is out of the papers and out of the public's thoughts. That is good, that will give us time to get everything and everyone in place. Just to add a little, we will use our connections with the media, to warn them to stay away from blackening the eye of an American hero by insinuating that he could possibly have anything to do with it. Nobody must be allowed, to even whisper, Jim's name. Perhaps we can use some of our political connections to direct the investigation. We will feed them some ideas. They will never know who we are protecting, even that we are protecting anyone. They must see it as our interest in seeing justice done to protect this land of ours from foreign interventionists." Mike laughed at Uncle Benny's pompous air as he said this. Then Mike said, "Well, Benjamin, I did not realize how eloquent you are." Uncle Benny laughed with him. They took a lunch break.

After lunch they started again. Uncle Benny was saying that the Cuban Americans who had lost loved ones in the Pig Bay fiasco could be possible targets for the redirection effort. Mike thought of Marta and the idea of setting something, he was doing onto her shoulders, was not appealing to him. He agreed that they could use it, but only if they had to, as a last resort.

Uncle Benny said, "Well, if not the Cuban Americans, how about that renegade who was the target of that invasion? He could have been angered enough to want to attack America, but knowing that he is no match for America, he instead goes after assassinating the man responsible for it." Mike liked the idea. It appealed to his sense of irony. Marta might still get some attack on that renegade in some very round about way. Perhaps her death was not completely in vain. "It would be nice if one of our patsies could have Cuban communist leanings," mussed Mike.

Mike added, "There are a lot of people right here in America who don't like what has happened. We will need to start the rumor mill about the possibility of disgruntled Americans doing it." Uncle Benny asked, "What else is going on lately?" Mike gave that a little thought and answered, "There is some stuff happening in French Indo

China that might develop into something. I don't think it is going anywhere soon if it goes anywhere at all. We have been helping France take back control of their colony after the Japanese were thrown out. There has been a group led by a guy named Ho Chi Minh trying to take control of their country back from the French. Maybe we could set up a patsy who is angry over the US intervention.

"When should it go down?" Asked Mike. Uncle Benny scratched his head and said, "I think we should wait for at least a year to pass. That will give the public a lot of time to forget about Lynn. Besides, who knows what will happen in a year. Presidents are always doing something to make someone mad. Maybe we will get lucky and find an opportunity to lay this at somebody else's feet."

We will put it all together and let the patsy controllers begin getting their patsies into the profile that we want them to have. We will look for some event that is to happen in a year's time and begin planning around that. I'll go to Washington to look around for a few good locations, "Mike said. "No!" Uncle Benny interjected, "We don't want to do it in Washington. For one reason, we don't have enough control over the situation in Washington. For another, the Secret Service has that town wired. Which is to say, they are prepared for someone to come into town who wants to take a shot at the President. If a foreigner wanted to kill the Pres., that is where they would go, to do it, and the Secret Service knows that. They have people all over that town, reporting to them about whatever they see or hear. They have game planned that whole town. They have already done what you are proposing to do and taken counter measures. Like I said, Washington is the wrong town to do this in.

Mike replied, "A proper site has to be reconned before it's usable. How do we do that on a moment's notice?" Uncle Benny said, "We have roughly a year to get ready. We know a lot about our target. He is high profile when he moves. When he moves around, he moves through large cities. Pick out an important city in each of the states. It should be either the political or economic center of the state. He won't miss visiting one or the other. Possibly, he will visit both centers. We don't have to visit all the states. Just pick out a dozen or less of the ones he is most likely to need to visit. In due course, he will be there, and we will have been there ahead of him." Mike added, "Of course! It's like hunting an animal, you don't have to know his every step, just know a few places where he is going to be and set up your blind. Like, his water hole. The animal may wander all over his territory, but he always comes back to his water hole. In this case, our target will need to keep in touch with his key people, in a few key cities, in a few key states. That's good! That makes the job a lot easier to manage.

I will build up a site analysis on each of the key cities and states to see if any of them can add some other element to help our profile." Uncle Benny added, "Remember, the larger the town, the more numerous the potential ambush sites. He would be traveling on the larger roads. Consider the presence of crowds. Because things change, don't pick out only one site in each town. He may use a different route than the one you think he will use and what was a good site one day may be totally different when you go back to do the job." Mike added, "The larger the town, the more places to hide, and the more numerous the escape routes, and the larger the crowds to get lost among and the greater the confusion." Uncle Benny added, "If, for whatever reason, we cannot do a safe hit in the town of our first choice, don't worry. He will be in one of the other towns, sooner or later. When he is, we will be ready and there before him. Mike asked, "I know the family has people in all these towns. Why don't we ask them to help us narrow the number of potential sites down? So that when I get to town I will only have to check out a handful of possible sites?" He had asked before he had thought it through. He caught himself while he was asking the question and answered it himself. "Of course! Of Course! I apologize for that lapse. Nobody, but us!"

CHAPTER XVI

MISSION

Uncle Benny spoke slower now, "Well, not quite, just us! There are going to be a lot of people playing their parts. There will be many people helping with rumors and the media. There will be people trying to steer the thinking of the police. There will be the patsy handlers. There will be a group of people who will cover your trail and set up false trails. There will be people planted in the crowd to give false reports of what they saw and heard. The more the true events are obfuscated, the less there is for the investigators to work on to build a true picture of what happened and how it happened. It is like giving them our duck hunting water holes. They can then set up blinds from which to ambush us. Therefore, conflicting reports from the event, will keep them from ever getting beyond the, guessing at possibilities, stage of their investigation. We will want to give them so many possible scenarios and possible suspects that they will be lost in their own office. The last thing we ever want is to be in court on this thing, but we will plan for it anyway. If there is a lot of conflicting evidence out there, then we can throw that up into the air and confuse the jury or at least put enough doubt in their minds so that they cannot, with any conviction, put us on the gallows."

Mike asked, "How are we going to coordinate all those people?" "We ain't!" Uncle Benny said, "You are going to take care of picking out the sites and your escape routes. On the day of the event you are the man. That is all that you are going to know. You have more on your plate than any man would want. I will take care of coordinating the other details. You know that you needn't worry about the other people, because you know that you can trust me to do the job right. It is important that you don't have anything else on your mind. It is important that you trust me completely. Everybody, involved with this will know only their job and that's all they will know. The vast majority of the people doing a part in this have no idea what they are a part of. After the job is done, they will be able to figure it out, but there won't be enough information on their plate to feed a bird. If you did take all their collective knowledge, about what happened, then someone could figure out how, but nobody would know why. I am the only person to know all the elements.

The only reason I'm telling you this much, is because when you are doing your part, you will need to be completely confident in the smooth operation of all the elements. If you are not, then perhaps you will have second thoughts at the wrong moment. Maybe you will get nervous about being caught. One nervous twitch on the trigger can send the whole mission into the can. I need to tell you enough so that you will have the calm assurance you will need to do the job right. Like I said, you have enough on your plate to take care of."

"Speaking of plates, let me introduce you to the best steak place in Lima. Big Joe has the best steaks. He calls his place Milanos. You have been eating my cooking and now you deserve something a bit better." Uncle Benny enjoyed eating out occasionally and when he did, he liked to eat steak.

In the car, on the drive back from the restaurant, Uncle Benny took a serious tone and said, "Mike, there is one more thing. It is important that you remember this. I am the one who knows everything and everybody. That means I need somebody to be my second, if anything goes wrong. If I cannot function, such as, let's say I have a heart attack or become enfeebled for whatever reason, go to Don Francis in St. Louis. Tell him I sent you. That's all! If, for some reason, 'God forbid', I should get picked up by the police, he will take care of me. You must disappear so completely and so fast that no one will ever find you. I have a safe in the house. There is a lot of money in it for emergencies. I will show you the combination when we get home. The other side of it is this Mike. If for whatever reason you cannot do this job; you get sick; you have a car accident, or if the police for any reason pick you up, then I am going to have to take care of you. You do know what I mean when I say; I will take care of you. Don't you?" Uncle Benny was looking earnestly, right into Mike's eyes and Mike understood what he meant. If Mike, so much as got drunk, and spent the night in jail, or spoke too loosely, Uncle Benny would have to kill him. It was just business-big business.

"When this is done Mike," Uncle Benny had assumed a lighter tone in his voice, "Whatever is in that safe is yours anyway. It will be your wages and you will need to try to find the edge of the world." Mike replied, that Uncle Benny might need some of it himself. Uncle Benny was silent for longer than Mike was expecting. When Uncle Benny did reply his voice was back to the serious tone. "Mike, I have a congestive heart. I think that is what the doctor called it. Earlier, you said I looked very healthy. Well, looks are deceiving. I have lived more years than either of my parents did. When I move, my joints ache. I don't have a sex life anymore. There is not anything I want to do after this job. I am tired Mike. I have about had it anyway. I look at some of those folks in their nursing homes or in the hospitals clinging to life at any length. Is that a life? I ask ya! Is that a life? No! No, it isn't any worthwhile kind of life. I don't want that for me. Life means having something to wake up for, something to wake up to. Whether it is a spouse, a loved one, or even a job, a person needs to have something besides just existence. Existence, bah! I don't want it. Besides, the one part of this job, that nobody else wanted, is the part that comes at the end of the job. I know too much to be allowed to live. If anyone of my people ever talks to anyone, then the police can follow the connection back to me, and through me to the whole enchilada. That cannot be allowed to happen. After you hit Collins, you need to take care of me. One thing I ask, I don't want to die in the street. I don't want to die like a cheap thug. Ok Mike?"

Mike tried to speak and found that his throat was unable to talk. He finally got out, "Sure, Uncle Benny! Sure! I will make everything right for you. You have my word on it."

"Thanks Mike! Thank you for being a good man." Uncle Benny's voice was back to being jovial again. "I always knew that you were a better man than most, a much better man. I could see that in you when you were still just a kid." The rest of the drive home was quiet.

A couple of weeks later the Russians began sending missiles to that renegade in Cuba. Uncle Benny damned the timing. "If they could have waited just another year." Remonstrated Uncle Benny. "That would have given us the kind of cover we need. It is still too soon after Lynn's murder. We don't even have our patsies lined up yet, and Collins is not moving around enough yet. Damn the luck!"

Mike was quietly thinking. Finally, he spoke, "It is ok! In fact, it is just about perfect. You see? If the Russians or the renegade were mad enough to hit the President. They could not do it yet for the same, or almost the same, reasons. They don't want to act so quickly that we would go to war over it. They have to wait for the same reasons we do, so that they can have plausible deniability. It works for both of us. We, the US, can think they did it, but because it is delayed we won't know for sure and then we won't be so apt to go to war. In addition to that, they would have the same infrastructure to put into place, as we do. Picking the sites, getting patsies in place, all that stuff. All the same problems we are looking at, they would be looking at." Uncle Benny perked up, "Yes! You're right! That's good, hey, that's good!" Then he laughed and said,

"What you will have to be careful of is, elbowing a Russian out of the way when you are ready to take your position. Ha, ha, ha! 'Get in line comrade, he is our President, we Americans get the first shot.' Ha, ha, ha!" Uncle Benny had not laughed this well for a long time. "And", Uncle Benny continued; "Now we have a wonderful curtain between Lynn's murder and the restoration of our honor." Uncle Benny was almost dancing as he moved into the kitchen for another cup of coffee.

That was the mental scene that Mike recalled while he was surreptitiously moving into his position. He almost wanted to ask out loud, "Hey! Any Ruskis here?" His attempt at humor, even in his own mind, helped him cope with the tension of the moment. He was all deadly serious in another part of his mind. He had gone into sniper positions and done the job many times in his career. This was what he had done for years in the service to his country. Now he was more nervous than ever before. He knew that it was because, while before he had the backing of the whole nation for his actions, now the whole nation would become his executioner. Ironic, he thought, he never before realized that what he had always thought of as a lonesome job, he had done with the moral strength that came from knowing that there was a huge number of people aware of and approving of his action even though the action would be in some remote part of the world where nobody, or very few anyway, would see the hit. Now, the world would know of the hit, and nobody would know whom or why, let alone approve of the action. Here, there would be hundreds of people around, yet, this time, he truly was alone.

He was also feeling a little vulnerable. He had always had a partner to cover his back. He knew that there was supposed to be someone, somewhere doing that for him, but he was not sure of him. He had always, before, known the capabilities of his partner. This working alone, in the dark, so to speak, not knowing the guy covering him, was uncomfortable.

It was time to clear his mind of all these thoughts. There he was and then it was done. No thinking allowed from here on out. He went into a type of meditation, a kind of trance. Where nothing was to distract him, not the cramped muscles, not the spider on his arm, not the sweat running down his nose, nothing. He was aware of everything, it was just that, nothing was important. His entire focus was on the target. All had to be blocked out, as though it were not even there. There was only room enough in his mind to calculate the wind shifting, the angle of declination and the movement of the target into the ranged distance.

He was out of the city before the deceased was declared dead. He drove straight through to Uncle Benny's house. He was wired. He was too agitated to sleep for the duration of the drive back. When he stopped for gasoline he drank strong coffee and drove on. He figured, he could sleep at Uncle Benny's for as long as he needed to let his nerves get back to normal. When the adrenaline came out of his system and the fatigue of driving caught up with him, his body would need to shut down for rest and rejuvenation. His mind would not be able to recognize danger quickly and his body would be slow to react. That is why when he drove up to Uncle Benny's house, at three o'clock in the morning, he was not alert. The light was still on in Uncle Benny's bedroom window. Mike figured that Uncle Benny had not been able to sleep either and he had waited up thinking that Mike would drive straight back.

When he went to the bedroom, the door was open. He spoke, "Good morning Ben!" and walked in. He saw Uncle Benny's body lying on the bed with a gun beside his hand and the side of his head blown off. The first thought to enter his mind was that Uncle Benny had wanted to spare Mike the grief of having to kill him. Mike figured that Uncle Benny would do that. How incredibly considerate of the old man. Before his thoughts took him farther, there was a voice behind him from the shadows. "Be cool! Don't move and you will live a little longer."

Mike didn't carry a gun. He was so exhausted that he did not trust himself to be able to physically disarm and neutralize somebody who probably did have a gun. Besides, the guy was smart enough to know where to stand. He was back in the shadows, behind him somewhere, and not too close. Mike spoke slowly, "Ok! I am cool! Do you want my wallet?" Mike didn't think it was a robber, but he wasn't going to tip his hand. The voice said, "I want you to sit down in that chair there with your back to me." As Mike moved into the chair he said, "Let me guess. He didn't shoot himself." The voice said, "Since I have the gun pointed at your back, I will ask the questions; got that?" Mike just said, "Ok!"

The voice asked, "Why does Don Francis want you and Benny knocked off? I have known Benny for a long time. Benny has been one of the most loyal guys in the entire organization. What did he do? And, who are you anyway? While I'm at it, stretch out your legs from the chair." Mike was puzzled by the last order. As he was stretching out his feet he asked, "What is this for?" The voice said, "From there, you cannot throw yourself out of the chair so quickly and try to get the jump on me. The extra time it takes for you to get your feet under you is enough time for me to react and plug you. Got it?" Mike didn't want to talk to anyone about the job, but he knew that Don Francis had sent this guy. He wasn't a robber or a cop. His mind was working slowly, but he knew he was about to end up like Uncle Benny. He could also figure why. "I see, so Don Francis was the one to give the job to Benny and now that the job is done, Don Francis wants all the possible connections back to him removed. It's insurance, and you are the claims adjuster."

The voice said, "Yeah, something like that. Don Francis told me that there would be somebody else coming by to see Benny. He even predicted that you would be coming by tonight. I was to wait for you. The Don didn't tell me who you are, so I would gather that he didn't know whom Benny would get for the job. How am I doing? I am right, aren't I?" Mike replied, "You better be looking over your shoulder now. If the Don is doing everybody who can connect him to the job, you could be next man to catch a bullet." The voice spoke, "Yes! That has occurred to me, but the Don doesn't know that I'm talking to you. He just told me to wait for you and to take you out. I'm sure he is expecting me to just bug out without asking you about why." Mike asked, "So, why are you asking questions? Why haven't you just done me and bugged out?"

The voice replied, "It is like I said, Benny never did anybody wrong. I will do what I have to do, but I want to know why and I know better than to ask Don Francis." Mike heaved a large sigh and shook his head. He was physically and mentally exhausted. He knew that he was going to die as soon as this guy in the shadows was satisfied. "Ok!" He said, "Do me a favor and I will tell you what has gone down. Ok?" The voice said, "I can figure part of it. There was some heavy action in Dallas yesterday. You arrive here exhausted, from a long drive. Don Francis wants one of his best men taken out. It does fall that way. Doesn't it?" Mike said, "You're right. Now, tell me that you will do me a favor and I'll fill in the blanks for you. Ok?" The voice said, "Ok!" Mike told him, "I am a retired Marine. I have always loved and served my country. Have somebody make the connections with the Corps. I want to be buried as a Marine who dedicated my life to the service of my country." "Done!" said the voice.

So, Mike began the story, "In the Corps, I was called Gunny Mike. In the family, I have been called Gunner Mike. Do you mind telling me who you are?" The voice replied, "I guess I do owe you that much. I'm called Young Joe. Don Francis would not be happy if he knew we were talking, but he won't find out. He showed up at my club a couple of days ago and gave me the assignment. He had to leave for L.A. right away to meet somebody." Mike interjected, "That would probably be Jim. They are probably drinking a toast to Lynn." Joe was surprised and said, "What?" Mike continued, "Let me explain. This thing we did; it wasn't for business. It wasn't for politics. It was for Jim. You see Collins had Lynn killed."

When Mike finished, Joe knew the whole story. "Wow," said Joe, "So, the President of the United States

Ben Romen

gets whacked for the oldest reason in the world. He fucked, dumped, and then killed somebody's woman. As they say in the old country, 'Un crime de passion.' And now, all the rest of this is just because that fucking, murdering bastard was the President. Shit! Now here I am, having to whack a guy like you. This really sucks." Mike quipped, "How do you think I feel about it?" "Right!" Joe added, "Well, look, if there were any other way, --business is business! I've got to do it. You understand!?" "Yes! I understand. All the loose ends, --and all that." That is all that Mike said. On the floor, some of Mike's blood flowed and mixed with Uncle Benny's blood.

CHAPTER XVII

TIME TO SAY GOODBYE

Mike had told Joe all that he knew about the operation. The money in the hidden safe did not cross his mind. He was a little distracted. Joe never knew about the money. Unless someone has done some major remodel on that house, it is probably still there, hidden deep in its structure somewhere.

Joe hustled out to the car. Dawn was not far from breaking. He woke up Leo and they drove straight back to New York. Joe was a lot more agitated than Leo had ever seen. Leo did not ask how it went. For one thing, it was not the thing to do. For two, he knew!

Leo had been half asleep, half awake, when Mike drove into the driveway of the house into which Joe had gone. Leo roused himself and when Mike went into the house. Leo went over to a window to cover Joe's back. He heard everything. He couldn't believe his ears. He realized that Don Francis was killing everyone who had a part in the assassination or even knew enough about it to bring the heat down on him. That meant that Joe too now, had to be careful. If Joe thought that Leo had heard, Joe might feel compelled to whack him also. Now Leo was starting to feel real vulnerable and nervous. He went back to the car and pretended to be asleep when Joe came out.

When they got back to New York, Joe told Leo that he was going to take a few days off. He was going to go upstate to do some fishing and unwind. "I'll call you when I get back." Leo said, "Sure Joe! See ya in a few days!" Leo went to the club and told Sammy that he and Joe were going to be gone for a few days. "Take care of things!" Then he picked up a bottle of Benchmark from behind the bar and went home.

Annie was feeling lonely in the evening and called the club to see if her boys had returned from their sudden and mysterious business trip. Sammy told her that they had returned and decided to take a few days off. Annie called Leo's apartment and when he answered, she knew he was drunk and worried about something. She went right over to see him and to try to take care of him.

Leo usually only had one drink in the evening before bed. Two drinks were for very special or unusual situations. The bottle of Benchmark was half empty. Annie could tell that Leo was way over his limit. She was shocked when she learned that the bottle had been new just a couple of hours earlier. "My God, Leo! What is wrong? What has happened? Why are you drinking so much? You can kill yourself if you're not careful." Leo laughed an evil laugh and said, "I might as well do it to myself before somebody else does." Annie was surprised by that reply. Leo had always been strong in his character and not one to be maudlin. "Talk to me Leo. Let me help." Leo said, "First, you better have a drink too. I don't think you want to know what I know." Then Leo did an affectation of a guy trying to act melodramatic. " I know what Joe knows, if Joe knows that you know what I know then I would have to kill you and then me too." Then he poured out a large drink for her and he topped off his glass again. He laughed and said, "We may as well get drunk and just let it happen, whatever is going to happen, because you just never know when you're going to wake up dead.

Annie was getting a little worried about the way Leo kept talking about dying. "Ok! I'll have a drink if you tell me what this is all about." "You've got a deal, sister. Just pour me another one while you're at it." Annie asked, "Haven't you had enough?" "I haven't had near enough to stop me from seeing what I saw and I haven't had enough to stop wondering who will be next." Leo said. "At least, if I get drunk enough, I won't care when it happens, if it happens." Ok!" Annie said, "Let's start somewhere, like at the beginning."

After Leo finished talking, Annie was too much in a kind of shock to believe what she had heard. Her whole world seemed to be a sand castle, which had just been hit by a large wave. She could not even get her mind to work for a while. She was almost stupefied. Her hands had gone from trembling to shaking. She had dropped her glass and did not seem to notice, let alone care. She couldn't stop saying, "My God! My God! Oh, my God!"

Then Leo started saying, "I don't know why I'm telling you this. I just have to tell somebody I guess. I

don't know what to do. I don't know if Joe knows that I
know or not. I don't think he knows, but I don't know.
Oh God! I sound like a comedy routine. That would be
funny for a comedian. For me, instead of getting laughter,
I might get dead. And now I've told you. My God! What
am I going to do about you? I know what the family
would say. I know what Don Francis would say. He would
say, "Business is business. Always take care of business
first. The man who doesn't take care of his business will
soon loose it to someone else who will take care of his
business for him. She is a lovely girl. Do her a good turn.
Don't let her know it's coming and do it without messing
up her face. If you like her, don't let her feel the knife. It is
more humane that way." Leo poured himself another one
and continued, "Yeah, I know what Don Francis would
say. Damn! Damn me for not being able to keep this to
myself. Now your life is in jeopardy too."

Leo drained his glass and turned abruptly to Annie
and grabbed her shoulders. "Annie! It is over between us.
Not only us, but also your whole life right now is gone. I
will stick around. Maybe Joe doesn't know. If he doesn't,
then I'll be ok. If he does, then I'm a dead man and you're
a dead woman. The only chance you have got is to go
away. Don't; just go to see your mama. If the family is
looking for you, there is no place they won't look for you.
You have to disappear completely. You will need a whole
new identity. That is easier for a woman. You have never
been in the military service or been fingerprinted. There
are no photos of you lying around. This might work for
you. Women change their names when they get married
all the time. You're a beautician. You work with hair
and cosmetics all the time. Change your look. Change

everything about yourself. Annie, it is your only chance to live. Go away and don't ever come back, not even for your mama's funeral, not for anything. Understand? God, Annie, you gotta understand. If I went away all of a sudden, then Joe would suspect and guess that I know something and my life wouldn't be worth a plug nickel. The only chance I've got is to stay here and ride it out. There is still a good chance that Joe doesn't know. You're going away can be explained. I will think of something. I will get somebody else lined up for the club. Annie, you have been a good woman to me. Thank you! I'm sorry, I've gotten you and your life so fucked up. Now go! Get out of here. I hope I never see your pretty face again. I'll miss you. Good-bye, Annie!

CHAPTER XVIII

AFTER ACTION REPORT

Don Francis was smoking a cigarette and drinking a glass of good Sicilian wine. As he gazed over the California landscape from the window of Jim's house, he began to muse, "You know Jim, I know that doing our thing requires a lot of sacrifices on the part of a lot of good people, but it is necessary. If we did not do what we do then the world would be completely under the control of men, who have no scruples at all. If that were ever to happen, life wouldn't be worth living for anyone. We would all be enslaved eventually to serving the almighty demigod, who would himself be serving his own lusts for power and wealth and control. As long as there are men, like us, who will not suffer these would be emperors; there will always be competition. A give and take in the lives of the average guy can give him hope to one day be able to get a little of the good life for himself.

We, by our activities, keep things in check. We balance the machine that runs this country.

Jim just grunted softly, and asked, "What about the brother?" Don Francis replied, "Now that his older brother is gone, he won't be able to do any harm. If it ever looks like he might get into a position to cause us a problem, then…" The Don just let his words trail off and he shrugged his shoulders as if to say, then we will take care of business.

Jim asked, "You are sure, there are no connections back to us." "Of course," replied the Don, "The whole deal was handled in the most professional manner. It is all over." Jim said, "I feel at odds with myself. I cannot let anyone know what I have done, but at the same time I yearn for people to know that I was not impotent to avenge Lynn's murder. That is only part of what bothers me. People don't know the truth about this guy. They don't know what he did to Lynn. I wish I could tell them what kind of bastard he really was.

The Don spoke up, "You know, I think it's ironic. That office, the Presidency. People confuse the office with the person and vice verse. If a man is killed, then the police look at the people who this man angered, cheated, or harmed. They are looking for a motive and will track back from that to find suspects. When a man is the President and he gets himself killed for what he has done as a man, then people look at what he has done as President. What I mean to say is that the investigation tries to see the motive for killing him differently. They don't think that he was killed for the same reasons that any other man would be killed for. They begin by suspecting the crazies who just want to shoot a President. Then they suspect the fringe political zealots. Then they suspect a foreign power. Do you see what I mean? They are focusing on what the President has or has done. They aren't looking at what the man has done. Because of this, and this is the part I think is ironic, the office shields him from due process of the law, but it also shields us from being the primary suspects. They are too busy looking at crazies, or renegades like Castro, or the Kremlin. They will never think to look at his personal behavior as something that caused his death."

Don Francis poured himself another glass of wine. Jim spoke up, "Lynn still wants people to know what he did to her." The Don looked at Jim. Jim spoke on, "I visit her grave regularly. I talk to her there. It is almost as though I can hear her in my thoughts. Maybe, I'm just going nuts, but I think she wants people to know the truth. I want people to know the truth about what he did to her. And I want people to know that I didn't allow him to get away with it."

The Don sipped his wine. He said, "I think it can all be handled in such a way that you can have both a full and free life and let the people know too." Jim turned and looked at the Don with a question in his face. Don Francis chuckled and continued, "Perhaps not while you are alive. Jim, live a good, full life and after you die, then the public can be told the story. Your public will understand your conflict and they will know." Jim asked, "Can you be sure of that?" The old Don smiled and said, "I guarantee it."

One week later, in the early hours of the dawn, a lone figure was seen visiting Lynn's grave. Jim had a dozen roses delivered to her grave every week. He was there, talking to her, as though she could really hear him. "Well

Lynn, I hope you can rest a little easier now. I thought I would, but the sad thing is, I cannot. I keep hearing this word, honor. I guess, maybe there was something to that, but they don't really understand. I never was any kind of honorable guy. I was just good at playing a game. That is the only thing I was ever any good at. You were the one who made me feel honorable. You made me feel wonderful. Baseball and the fans made me feel successful. The game made me rich, but it was you who made me feel like a king. You were the only person who ever really knew and understood me. You were the only person to ever really, and completely, love me, the man. I did this, because he made me mad. It made me mad, the way he led you on with his empty promises of marriage. Leading you away from me. It made me mad the way he, they, all of them, abused your kindness. Then, to go and kill you was too much. I was angry and I did this only because, when you entered my life, you entered my heart. I love you."

EPILOGUE

Annie and I are expecting our first grandchild in May. We were married six months after she told me her story. I don't know what happened to Leo or Joe. I hope I never know. I am still working as a welder in the oil construction business, but these days I work only on land where I can have my family near me. When one refinery is completed we move on to the next new job. We are called travelers, tramp workers in the industrial construction business. We move from job to job and travel all over the world. We get to see a lot of interesting places that other people only read about. It is not a glamorous life, but it is an honest one. We sleep well.

This story can now be told. All the lead characters are dead. How can you know if it's true? All you can do is — trust me.

We dedicate this, their story, to them.

To John, who wants us to know who really is responsible for his murder.

To Joe, who wants us to know that he was not impotent to avenge the murder of his wife when no one else would or could.

To Marilyn, who wants us to know that she did not commit suicide and that her Joe always was her champion.

Ben Romen